DEAD ON COURSE

DEAD ON COURSE

J. M. Gregson

Chivers Press   G.K. Hall & Co.
Bath, England   •   Waterville, Maine USA

LT M Gregson

This Large Print edition is published by Chivers Press, England, and by G.K. Hall & Co., USA.

Published in 2002 in the U.K. by arrangement with the author.

Published in 2002 in the U.S. by arrangement with Juliet Burton Literary Agency.

U.K. Hardcover   ISBN 0–7540–4754–7 (Chivers Large Print)
U.S. Softcover   ISBN 0–7838–9672–7 (Nightingale Series Edition)

The text of this Large Print edition is unabridged.
Other aspects of the book may vary from the original edition.

Set in 16 pt. New Times Roman.

Printed in Great Britain on acid-free paper.

British Library Cataloguing in Publication Data available

Library of Congress Cataloging-in-Publication Data

Gregson, J. M.
    Dead on course / J.M. Gregson.
       p.   cm.
    ISBN 0–7838–9672–7 (lg. print : sc : alk. paper)
    1. Police—England—Hereford—Fiction. 2. Hereford (England)—Fiction. 3. Golfers—Fiction. 4. Large type books.
I. Title.
PR6057.R3876 D43 2002
823'.914—dc21   2001039974

MONDAY

CHAPTER ONE

'Sod and damnation!' said Guy Harrington.

It is a truth universally acknowledged among golfers that water attracts golf balls. The immortal Miss Austen would certainly have noted that, had she lived a century later, for the acuteness of her observation would undoubtedly have drawn her to this most revealing of games.

Harrington's well-struck three-iron looped in a beguiling parabola, seeming to stay in the air for an inordinately long time as it sliced inexorably to the right of his target. Then it landed in the river with a silent splash, visible to all four members of the match but too distant for the sound to carry to them. Harrington gave vent to his feelings with a renewed and more lurid verbal outburst.

His companions tried to control the smiles which are always provoked by other people's sufferings in this game. Even Harrington's partner in the four-ball, Tony Nash, felt quite cheerful about his man's discomfort, for it allowed him to feel less guilty about his own incompetence earlier in the round, which Harrington had received with ill-concealed irritation. Being a tycoon seemed to make a

1

man less tolerant of the weaknesses of his underlings, even when they were officially at play together. Nash called an unconvincing 'Hard luck, Guy,' to the man stamping heavily towards the bank of the Wye and went forward to his own ball.

Nash, concentrating fiercely beneath his luxuriant fair hair, managed to get to the green in three, but then three-putted; Harrington watched him with massive, unbelieving disapproval. Sandy Munro, as slight and pale as Harrington was bulky and florid, chipped up deftly from the edge of the green and holed without fuss for a four to win the hole.

The Scotsman was forty-six, but had the same waist and weight he had had at eighteen; his red hair and blue eyes were almost as bright as in the days of his youth. His slender build concealed surprising strength; where the other three pulled trolleys, he carried a full bag of clubs without effort. He had been a golfer for almost four decades of those forty-six years. Before he was twenty, there had been talk of his turning pro, but he was too good an engineer and his parents too imbued with Scottish caution to allow that. He had been among the Sassenachs in the south of England now for twenty years losing neither his soft Fifeshire accent nor his golfing skills: he maintained his handicap of two with no hint of concession yet to the advancing years.

The result was that in a game notoriously

unpredictable, Sandy Munro's four had an air of routine, the execution that of well-oiled, repeating skills. His partner, George Goodman, said, 'Well done, Sandy, two up with three to play!' It had the sound of a recurrent, unthinking chorus, though it made no sweeter hearing for his opponents for that.

Goodman, as unconscious of their irritation as the unworldly bishop he resembled physically, teed his ball carefully and dispatched it down the exact centre of the fairway, with a precision wholly inappropriate to his generous handicap. He held his position at the top of his follow-through in the manner beloved of amateurs the world over after a good shot, while his opponents muttered again about his eighteen handicap and the unfairness of it all.

But in truth, it was only mock war and synthetic indignation. Among friends in such a setting, anything else would have been quite stupid—and none of these men was stupid. Oak and beech stood around them in the full emerald glory of their early leaf. As the course turned back towards the clubhouse, the Wye wound serenely away to their left, still as a painted river as afternoon moved into evening. Some men are foolish enough to quarrel in places like this, but not all men. These four had come away for a week's golf and fun, and the golf must increase rather than diminish the fun.

They had known each other for many years now, on and off the golf course; they had learned to make the small adjustments necessary to each other's idiosyncrasies. They were not intimate friends perhaps; in one case in particular there was little affection extended from any of them. But they knew how to rub along together happily enough, in that bluff, undefined male way that understood just how far they should intrude into each other's lives.

Their relationships would not have stood the test of greater intimacy; at the end of this week they would go back to their normal lives of work and home with a certain secret relief that they did not have to exist permanently in the close proximity of these golfing days. But any strain they felt this week was submerged in the pleasure of their activities. Save, that is, for one of them, who never ceased his endeavours to gather information which might be of use to him.

As the end of the round approached, all was good fellowship and breezy banter. When Guy Harrington, lurching into the ball with characteristic vehemence on the sixteenth, won the hole with the four which was always a possibility of his eccentric game, even his opponents were glad for him, and pleased at the prospect of the game going all the way to the last green. George Goodman, silver hair setting off a becoming bald dome, retrieved his opponent's ball carefully from the hole and held it between finger and thumb as delicately as a Eucharist wafer. He handed it to Harrington with a congratulatory smile. 'Whose handicap's too high now, then?' he said.

'A one-off, George! A flash in the pan. You know my game well enough!' said Harrington modestly. But his expression denied the words: the realism which informed his business decisions deserted him as soon as he got hold of a club, so that he thought his finest shots represented his normal game, instead of recognizing them as the splendid aberrations they were. In other words, he was a typical golfer. There is no game in which hope so consistently outstrips performance.

Tony Nash produced the longest drive of the four at the seventeenth, as befitted his broad shoulders and tender years: he was a mere forty-two, with hair long and luxuriant enough to provoke heavy-handed jokes about barbers' estimates around golf clubs, those bastions of sartorial conservatism. He thinned his second shot, but it ran low and straight, bouncing merrily on to the green while he tried not to catch the eye of Sandy Munro. He holed the putt for an unlikely three; an afternoon which had been full of frustration for him suddenly seemed idyllic.

All square. They climbed the eighteenth's steep elevation to the clubhouse and watched Sandy Munro almost win the match with a curling putt which lipped the hole but refused to drop. A halved match, then. They shook hands, going through a ritual ridiculous in friends who had been together for two days and planned to be so for another three.

Telling each other it was the right result, the four men stood contentedly for a moment beside the clubhouse, able for the first time now to give their full attention to the appealing scene below them. The ground dropped away steeply, so that they could see many of the last nine holes they had just played. Other golfers were visible at various stages of their rounds, but they were too distant for their voices to disturb the serenity of a scene which had changed little for centuries.

A field of oil-seed rape seemed in the evening light an even more vivid yellow; the only moving things visible in the wide panorama on the other side of the river were a highly animated black labrador and its less energetic master. From a distant cottage, a thin blue line of smoke rose straight as a pole towards the blue above. The river was a central feature in a landscape as balanced as if it had been planned by a painter. From this height, its graceful course could be followed for miles. At its widest bend, the descending sun lit its surface with a golden fire; elsewhere, it was as dark and quiet as if it had been frozen in a photograph.

The Wye Castle Golf and Leisure Complex boasted in its brochure that many of its rooms looked out over the course and the river. In one of these, a striking red-haired woman watched unseen what was happening below her. The window commanded an excellent view of the pastoral English scene, but she had eyes only for the four men on the last green. As they left the course and moved to stow away their trolleys and clubs, she watched them intently.

It was impossible to have any idea which of the four in particular commanded her unblinking gaze. What was unmistakable was the hatred, harsh and undiluted, with which she watched him.

CHAPTER TWO

The building at the centre of the Wye Castle complex was not a castle, of course. The occasional visitor arrived and departed feeling that the Wars of the Roses had probably clashed around these walls and Cromwell's cannons must surely have been discharged from the valley below, but few were as naïve as that.

It was no more than a pleasant eighteenth-century mansion, distinguished chiefly by the superb position of its escarpment above the river. The nineteenth-century owner, under the influence of the mediaevalism of the romantic poets and the more questionable suggestions of the Gothic novel, had added the castellations and the random turrets. These not only ruined the original Georgian simplicity of the design but caused expensive problems of maintenance, once the estate ceased to employ its own builders and carpenters and men ceased to be cheaper than horses to maintain.

Floodlit against a starry sky, the ivy-clad elevations of this mongrel building had a brooding menace that suggested *Psycho* more than Childe Roland. But the interior was cheerful enough. Well-lit and warm behind its velvet curtains, with the ubiquitous musak discreetly low, the bars and dining-room felt welcoming enough, even though in May they were almost empty.

The arrival of Guy Harrington's party, full of group confidence and determined bonhomie, made the impact of a much larger presence upon this quiet place. It was Harrington, well accustomed to authority, who took control, seeing to the seating of the ladies and discussing the choice of wine with the air of a host. If there was any resentment among his audience, there was no visible sign of it: perhaps they were happy to see someone with much experience of these things taking control on their behalf. Or perhaps, after a full day of physical activity, they were enjoying that delicious lassitude that takes over at the prospect of good food and pleasant company.

The two women felt at least as tired as the four men. Sightseeing can be more exhausting than golf. And when you cannot quite agree what you wish to see, and yet are too polite to go your separate ways, you end up doing too much. They had spent two absorbing hours in the Cathedral at Gloucester, guided round its ancient glories by a well-mounted exhibition of its history. Alison Munro could have spent much longer, but her friend had been impatient to visit the shops, where they had spent most of an afternoon which had begun to seem interminable. She had spent the last hour of it studying a beguiling square of blue sky through the single high window of a fitting room, while Meg Peters tried on a succession of dresses and rejected them all.

Alison was the only wife there. Two of the other men had wives, but they had opted out of the boozy gaiety and interminable golf talk and stayed at home; perhaps they felt that a single wife in attendance was sentry enough to ensure propriety in their men. Alison eased off her elegant high-heeled shoes beneath the table, careful not to play unwitting footsy with any hopeful male. She let her smile glitter freely at some minor witticism from her left. But it was the liberation of her throbbing feet which almost made her grunt with unladylike relief.

From her name, she should have been as Scottish as her husband, but she was pure English for as far back as anyone could trace, which was at least two centuries of Berkshire gentry. Her mother, having to cope with a surname of Browne, which even the additional 'e' could scarcely dignify, had merely thought the sound of the name Alison attractive and the three syllables a suitable counterbalance to the surname.

Alison Munro had never needed to rely upon her name for interest. With the type of beauty that used to be characterized as that of an English rose and a seat on a horse as proud as any queen's, she had turned many a rich head, and even several titled ones. When she had chosen to throw in her lot with the physically undistinguished and conversationally inept young engineer from Perthshire, who had never been inside anything so grand as a drawing-room before he met her, there had been much shaking of heads. But those heads had underestimated both of them.

She flashed a conspiratorial smile at Sandy, two places away from her at the end of the table. Harrington, who had been relishing the gloss of her jet-black hair, sculpted so becomingly round that poised head, and wondering if its lustre could owe anything at all to the artifice of the bottle, intercepted the look and felt his intrusion. How boring goodness was, he thought; how much more interesting and varied were the possibilities of old-fashioned sin.

Whether it was this thought which prompted him to look at the other woman in the party, he was not sure. Meg Peters certainly provided a physical contrast. She was nine years younger than Alison's forty-three, slim and elegant, conscious of her powers. Her features had not the older woman's classical regularity. But she had soft green eyes of proven potency; at close quarters they were almost hypnotic when she chose that they should be. Her most remarkable feature from any greater distance was her hair. Long and luxuriant, it was a most remarkable chestnut red, seeming to change its hue and its density as the light caught it at different angles.

She was here with Tony Nash. Both had been married before: she was divorced, he was separated. Nash had had a bad day on the golf course, until his late flowering, and there had been male sympathy for him there. As he came into the room with Meg Peters, there was male envy.

Harrington and Goodman had single rooms, but they had met for a Scotch before dinner. Guy had enlarged enviously upon the 'wall to wall crumpet' denied to them and supposedly enjoyed by their companions. Goodman had smiled weakly and retired to ring his wife before the meal.

The lighting around the tables was designed to flatter beauty past its first bloom, though these two women scarcely needed its aid. There was just enough illumination through pink shading to supplement the candles the waiter lit as they studied the menu. Soft light glittered on glass and cutlery, adding to the pleasurable anticipation already induced by sharp appetite. With the restaurant so quiet, they accepted George Goodman's suggestion to avoid the more exotic items unless they were prepared to accept the dubious flavours of the deep freeze. The beef proved good; the claret, if not the finest, was acceptable enough at the price. For a while, the conversation grew sporadic as the knives worked busily and the bottles and vegetable dishes did the rounds.

No one was quite sure afterwards how the row began. There were separate conversations around the table, which perhaps distracted from the conflagration until it had burst into full flame. The first indication that most of them had of trouble was Tony Nash's melodramatic, 'Either you take that back immediately or you'll be sorry!'

It was so much of a cliché that some of them thought at first it was mere parody. It took Nash's harsh, uneven breathing to convince them that the words were serious. In the sudden, embarrassed silence which fell upon the table, it sounded unnaturally loud, announcing his emotion more clearly than his words.

Harrington's laugh took a second too long to come. When it did, it sounded as stagey as the younger man's challenge. Like a chuckle from Mr Punch as he raised his stick, it was aimed at the audience rather than his victim. His smoothly jowled face was florid, almost purple in the rosy light. How much was due to sun and fresh air, how much to wine and emotion, none of them could have said at that moment. He said, 'Oh, come on, Tony, don't be stupid! You know perfectly well I was joking.' His voice was just unsteady enough for his words to lose conviction.

'I know damn well you weren't! And so do you!' Nash's anger gave the banal words a weight they should not have had. Not a dignity: men brawling in a restaurant can never have that. But his blazing sense of grievance gave him an odd kind of integrity: for the first time that any of his audience could remember, he was speaking to the older man without the awareness of him as an employer.

Meg Peters put her hand softly on top of Nash's broader one as she saw it quivering with rage. 'Let it go, Tony,' she said quietly. So the insult, whatever it had been, had been to her. Alison Munro was assailed by the uncharitable but accurate female reaction that Meg was a woman well able to look after herself. How ridiculous and impractical these men became once they began to strike poses!

13

Nash shook his lover's hand aside almost angrily, as if it were an insect disturbing his concentration. For a moment the two men glared at each other angrily, like boys in a school playground. Then the older man shrugged. 'If you are annoyed, Tony, of course I withdraw my remark. I'm sure the fair Meg understands that no offence was intended.' He turned upon Ms Peters a smile that was meant to be dazzling but which emerged in its extravagance as merely false.

The others seized on the opportunity to end an embarrassing incident. Soothing words were applied like ointment; within two minutes, the buzz of different conversations was resumed emolliently around the big table. The waiters went back into the kitchen to discuss the tensions of Home Counties emotions with the chef. The two other diners in the room resumed their whispered conversation and pretended they had not even noticed the cabaret in the centre of the room. Only Tony Nash, staring unseeing at his dessert, obstinately preserved the moment the others had banished.

By the time they retired to the adjoining lounge for coffee, the atmosphere was almost restored. Nash, treasuring his grievance in silence, replying with monosyllables to those who sought to divert him, appeared an unlikely, even a slightly ridiculous champion. This was partly because his damsel seemed far too sophisticated to be in any real distress. Watching Meg Peters smiling and unruffled, telling against herself the story of her ridiculous indecision over dresses earlier in the day, it was difficult to see her as vulnerable enough to necessitate the raw passion of Nash's recent defence.

Later, replete with good food and wine, they sat with liqueurs on the flat roof at the top of the old building. It was a still, velvety night, which they were reluctant to leave. The stars and a slim crescent of moon meant that they could just catch the great curve of the river, silver in the distance as it had been since before the days of man. As if cued by the balmy warmth, a nightingale sang below them in the woods by the river, the remote, ethereal beauty of its notes stilling the sporadic exchanges of the human company above.

When they at last broke up, it was after midnight. Sandy Munro, who had rarely sat still for so long at a stretch, strolled alone through the night down the Wye Castle drive to the distant gates. The drive was almost three-quarters of a mile long; his practical mind diverted itself for a while with the cost of resurfacing it. For much of its length it was flanked by an avenue of two-hundred-year-old limes. Towards the gates, there was some undergrowth beneath these; the myriad scratchings of nocturnal wild life as he approached were unnaturally loud in the

15

prevailing silence. He strolled over to the nearest green. He had been on thousands of golf greens in the last forty years, but never one by moonlight. The turf was soft as carpet beneath his feet, seeming in this light even more immaculately manicured than by day. The innocent place, so obviously manmade amid the natural features dimly visible all around him, seemed in its artificial rectitude almost threatening: it had the groomed, eerie stillness of a well-kept grave. With the thought, he turned and walked more briskly back towards the dark outlines of the main house and the lower shadows of its newly built accommodation lodges.

As he entered the gravelled courtyard which was surrounded by the apartments, he heard the muffled sound of voices raised in argument. The flat roof was deserted now; the voices came from somewhere beneath it. At first, he thought Harrington and Nash had renewed their quarrel, and his spirits drooped at the thought of the implications for the rest of their week here. Then it seemed to him that the voices were male and female. He wondered if Meg Peters and Tony Nash were arguing about the vehemence of his reaction earlier in the evening. But there were other people staying here as well as their party, he reminded himself.

He let himself quietly into his own room. To his surprise, it was empty. He hardly realized

16

how much he relied on the comforting presence of his wife in all he did; perhaps he did not want to acknowledge such dependence. But he was not seriously disturbed.

Alison's absence did not at the time seem significant.

TUESDAY

CHAPTER THREE

George Goodman had a disturbed night.

Although it had been late when he crept between the sheets, he woke from an uneasy sleep to the sound of the dawn chorus. It began with a solitary thrush and swelled to a massive avian outburst as the different species added their contributions to the rich and varied sound, and he heard every detail. He knew now that he had overdone himself; he wasn't as young as he used to be. On those mournful thoughts, he turned away from the light and tried desperately to sleep.

Two hours later he accepted dolefully that there was no more rest for him. He sat on the edge of the bed for a moment, then padded through his first arthritic groans to the thin flowered curtains, drew them back, and surveyed the scene. Clear blue sky; the sun invisible somewhere to his right, but gilding the trees with its low morning rays. No human presence that he could see; rabbits busy at their eccentric play on the edge of the woods a hundred and fifty yards away. Whether God was in his heaven was debatable, but all seemed well in what he could see of the world.

He set the electric kettle in the corner of the room to make tea, then shaved carefully with soap and water in the neat little bathroom. He looked with some distaste at the bishop's face that others found so benign. He had not always looked like this. It was middle age which had whitened his hair and tonsured his dome: within this benign clerical figure he felt a lively and lustful young blood trying ineffectively to avoid eclipse. Why couldn't the mind and the body keep more effective step with each other on their march through life? He sipped his tea and wondered how many more springs he would see.

It was an unwelcome reflection, arriving unannounced to a mind that had not prepared defences against it. But at least it prompted him into activity, perhaps in an attempt to keep unwelcome reflections at bay. Through his window, he caught a glimpse of the most unlikely early riser in their party. With an abstracted air, Tony Nash, his yellow hair in uncharacteristic disarray, was wandering towards the course and the low eastern sun.

Goodman went outside and sniffed the cool,

clear air appreciatively. This was always the best time of day in spring and summer—once one had made the effort to get up and dressed. His days as a village boy in Norfolk came vividly back to him. Was it really half a century since those days when he had trailed behind farm labourers, who had seemed to his wide small boy's eyes so magnificently, impossibly strong?

He stalked his man softly, enjoying seeing him start when he called from ten yards or so behind him, 'Glad to see someone else couldn't sleep either!'

Tony Nash looked even worse than George felt. His eyes were dark with lack of sleep beneath the dishevelled hair, his clothing in uncharacteristic disarray. He followed Goodman's gaze, looked down and tucked away the light blue leisure shirt that was half in and half out of the band of his trousers. 'Thought for a moment my flies must be undone!' he said.

'You're obviously not a morning person,' said George. 'I don't think I am, any more.' They walked without further exchange around the edge of the bowling green, watching the dew sparkling as the low sun began to burn it off. Nash, versed in the ways of the city, checked automatically that his car had not been stolen overnight. The movement gave Goodman an idea. Their clubs were in the cars. 'What about a few holes before

19

breakfast?' he said.

Nash was lighting a cigarette and he half-expected him to refuse. Instead, the younger man accepted the suggestion eagerly. He looked exhausted, as though he had slept even less than Goodman, but he was full of a feverish energy which sought outlet in movement. In three minutes, they had their bags and trolleys out of the cars and were standing by the first tee.

The course stretched appealingly before them, waiting to be conquered. Not a soul was in sight; there was just enough light breeze to flutter the distant flags and remind them that it was still not long after six. Their opening drives were well struck and bounced appealingly over the generous width of the first fairway. The world seemed a pleasing place, and they quite privileged within it.

It could not last, of course. It did not take long for fallibility to creep into their play, and they played their usual quota of shots from rough and sand as they went along. But on a morning like this, playing without hindrance at their own brisk pace, it mattered less than usual. The only loud noise in their first hour was the call of a skein of wild geese over their heads at the highest part of the course. The two men watched the geese until they were almost invisible, studied for a moment the distant tower of the cathedral at Hereford as it emerged from the morning haze, and congratulated themselves upon their presence here at such an hour.

As they played the eighth, two other residents crept sleepily on to the adjacent first tee, looking in awe at these two free-striding Titans who had been so far in front of what they had thought an early rising. Then there came the sound of the greenkeeper's tractor moving from its shed within a copse of cedars; it must have been half a mile away, but it sounded unnaturally near in the prevailing silence. Soon they reached the part of the course that ran above the river, and a group of eight glistening black labrador puppies provided them with much free entertainment as they ran in and out of the water on the far bank, shaking themselves enthusiastically around their philosophical owner.

Tony Nash was the only smoker in the party of six. He must have worked his way through the bulk of a packet over their first nine holes; George Goodman had not realized that he was so heavy an addict. He twitted Tony about it as they went, with the cheerful self-righteousness of the reformed sinner; he had not touched tobacco now for seven years.

Despite his smoker's pallor and his unusually unkempt appearance, Nash was striking the ball quite well. They agreed that they would play to the twelfth, conveniently near the clubhouse, and adjourn for breakfast. Tony Nash looked forward to the bacon and eggs and the feeling of complacent virtue he would enjoy when eating among those who had not yet set foot outside on such a morning.

The shout came as they were completing the eleventh. Away to their left, beneath the shadow of a huge beech, a young greenkeeper waved at them a frantic, unsteady arm. He stood on the edge of a small hollow in the ground, which had been an ancient dewpond before the area was drained to make the course. He had moved there to empty his cuttings after mowing the adjacent green: the mower box still dangled awkwardly from his left hand while he gesticulated with his right.

They covered the hundred and fifty yards to the spot at no great speed, for the ground was uneven and they were beginning to feel the need of food to revive their flagging energies.

And indeed, haste could have had no effect upon the thing that awaited them. They took in the young man's white face, the limbs unco-ordinated with shock, the voice that would not form words as he tried to explain his distress.

Behind him, invisible until they entered the hollow, the body lay awkwardly across a small mound, like a boxer splayed unconscious across the bottom rope of a ring. It lay face upward, and that face was unnaturally dark, almost black in places. But it was the eyes which caught and held the attention. Wide and dark, with the pupils fully dilated, they stared unseeingly at the bright sun. Neither

Goodman nor Nash felt any urge to move forward and close them.

Guy Harrington was very dead indeed.

CHAPTER FOUR

'Bloody golfers! What else can you expect from them but trouble?' Sergeant Hook spoke with gloomy satisfaction, as if a single outburst of foul play among the patrons of the Wye Castle justified all his formidable prejudice against this absurd game.

John Lambert drove the big Vauxhall carefully up the long drive and looked enviously at the placid green acres of undulating fairways beside him. Unlike the cricket enthusiast beside him, he played golf, and this was a morning to coax out even the rustiest swing. The sun was high now; they felt its warmth on their backs, even through the jackets of their suits, as they walked between the high walls of the hotel and the new residential lodges.

They had no difficulty in identifying the place. Already the screens had been erected around the hollow where the body had been discovered. The Scene of Crime team were being briefed by Detective-Sergeant Johnson; in the face of a Superintendent arriving to take formal control of the case, they parted like the

Red Sea to allow him entry to the enclosure of death.

Lambert had been in court; he was later arriving here than he would have liked. He had an illogical, egocentric suspicion that he could spot something others might miss if he could be at the scene before hundreds of other feet trampled the area. The young PC with the clipboard looked anxiously towards the Scene of Crime Officer at the approach of top brass. Morris nodded and he recorded Lambert and Hook beneath the other names on his list, his careful hand shaking only a little as he wrote. If suggestive footprints or fingerprints were found around the body, theirs as well as others' would need to be eliminated.

Resignedly, Lambert donned a disposable white paper overall and overshoes. Much as he might mumble about resembling an astronaut instead of the detective he had been when he joined the CID twenty years ago, he knew the strange accoutrements would prevent him from contaminating the area with his own fibres and dust.

He watched the police photographer take the last of his pictures of the body *in situ*. Then he moved down the narrow path between the white plastic tapes to inspect what had recently been Guy Harrington. He looked down at the corpse dispassionately, too well versed in the appearances of death to flinch from those wide, unseeing eyes that would never blink again. There was an old superstition that the eyes of the dead retained the image of the last thing they had seen in life. If only that were so! He stood for a moment without speaking, watching the careful movements of the silver-haired man who crouched beside the corpse.

'Here before you, for once, John.' It was the first moment when Lambert knew that the pathologist was aware of his presence. 'Very interesting.'

Lambert sighed: he knew exactly what those words presaged. 'Natural causes?' he inquired, without any feeling of hope. He had already seen the great patch of blood from temple to neck on the left side of the head, almost black now that it had been dried to a thick crust by sun and breeze. Tiny specks of gravel were trapped amid the congealed gore, peeping out of the sticky surface like nuts on the top of a fruit cake. Wisps of dried grass, trapped in the wound as it dried, moved gently in response to the light wind; an insect crawled unchecked over the matted hair. So soon did a living man, who had yesterday responded to the world around him, become an object with less volition than a fly.

'Oh, I doubt this one is natural causes!' said Burgess with relish. He rebuttoned the single shirt button he had gingerly undone on the thing beneath him. He intoned in the manner of what he took to be an official police announcement, 'Foul play is certainly suspected.' He rose from his preliminary examination of the remains and turned the blandest of smiles on Lambert. He was an erect figure still, despite being now around sixty. He looked round the twenty or so people within earshot to check that there were no relatives or media representatives, then said in his most bloodthirsty manner, 'I shall be more certain when I have cut him up on my friendly slab.'

Lambert thought he could scarcely imagine a place less friendly than the mortician's workshop where Burgess was in his element. It had the abattoir accompaniments of the operating theatre—the gleaming instruments of incision, the sterile metres of stainless steel, the channels to sluice away streams of blood— without the hope of prolonging life which was the hospital's ultimate redemption. Burgess had dabbled with surgery in his youth; Lambert recalled his contention that only pathology had afforded him the unhurried conditions, the chance to pursue and confirm his findings, which his tidy scientist's mind demanded. The dead felt no pain, and they were never in a hurry.

Lambert looked around at the men beginning to comb the area systematically, the photographer putting away his equipment, the plain van easing its way slowly over the turf from where the road ended by the clubhouse. He was the centre, the controller, of all this activity. That was a situation that would have been reserved for his fantasies when he set out on the paths of detection. There was enough of the old Adam in him for him to savour the thought.

He could never voice it, not even at home; especially not at home. Christine, to whom ambition and status were the most ridiculous of human pretensions, would mock him mercilessly for it. He looked down again at the thing which had provoked all this activity. 'Beaten to death with your old favourite the blunt instrument?' he said.

Burgess was not at all put out by the Superintendent's view that he read far too much crime fiction. He pursed his lips, deliberately prolonging the moment he had looked forward to. 'It's possible. Unlikely though, I'd say. Be able to tell better when you let me get his clothes off and take a proper look at him. Would you like me to thicken the plot a little for you, even at this early stage?'

'No, I wouldn't. But I presume you have a complication to report.'

'You could call it that, I suppose. You're more prosaic than I am: I prefer to see it as a thickening of the plot. You noticed the blackening of the face and the palms, no doubt?'

Lambert nodded. He had assumed bruising until now, though perhaps he should have known better. Because suddenly he knew what

Burgess was going to say.

'I won't hazard a guess about the cause of death yet. That wound on the side of the head looks nasty. But it wouldn't kill a man, of itself. I think there are fractures, but I didn't want to remove any clothing until you and your team had finished here. The really interesting thing is that blueing of the skin on the face and forehead; I've just stolen a look at the chest and the same effect is quite clear there. For some considerable time after he died, this chap was lying face downwards.'

Bert Hook, who was less squeamish about these things than his chief, looked at the corpse and the ground around it with renewed interest. 'So someone came back and turned him over, several hours after his death?' He looked for the outline of a corpse in the rough grass of the hollow, began calculations about the heaviness of the overnight dew.

'Or dumped him here after he had been killed somewhere else,' said Lambert. The three of them turned automatically to look over the heads of the bent figures who were systematically combing the area around them. The old house was in bright sunlight now, with high white clouds moving slowly above it, but from two hundred feet below, its ivy-clad gothic elevations still suggested hidden horrors and sinister passions.

Burgess looked back at the man at the centre of this mystery. The corpse had that look of superiority which seemed often to descend upon victims of violence, as if they were full of knowledge they could never now reveal. 'I'd guess at something not far off fifteen stone,' he said. 'It would take a strong man to carry him here.'

'Or two determined women. Or some form of transport,' said Lambert. He looked at the smooth green turf between them and the residential complex. 'The ground is always hard when you're looking for signs of wheel tracks.' But if anyone had come that way with a dead weight as heavy as the one beside them, he would surely have left some trace.

He took a last look at the body of Guy Harrington, splayed so awkwardly across the hump of turf, his stomach pointing at the sky in a pose he could not have held for long in life. If he had been dumped rather than fallen here, this odd disposition of the limbs was explained. It was the last time he would see him thus, and he left the site with a familiar regret, as if unlimited time to himself here would tell him things about this death which would otherwise take much hard digging among the living. It was no more than a superstition, to which a rational man could not even admit. He went over to the driver of the waiting van. 'You can remove him as soon as the Scene of Crime Officer is satisfied,' he said.

The three men walked silently back towards

the lodges, each busy with his own thoughts. Detective-Inspector Rushton, Lambert's deputy, was waiting for them there. 'Murder Room here, sir? There's plenty of accommodation—the place is much less than half full at present.'

Lambert nodded. 'It looks as though he didn't die where he was found. Make sure the whole area around the house is searched thoroughly before the public are allowed back.'

Rushton said with satisfaction, 'Already in hand, sir. If he died here, we should know where by the end of the day. By the looks of him, there should be blood somewhere.'

Lambert found himself wishing Rushton were not so consistently ahead of him. It was petty: the DI was efficient and enthusiastic, and he had already been here for three hours. He said more sharply than he intended, 'And look for something on which the corpse might have been transported. If we're right that the body has been moved, I doubt whether he was taken out there on someone's shoulders.'

Rushton said, 'I've already cordoned off the cars. The Scene of Crime team will have someone on to them within the hour.'

'A car is the obvious thing, but a lot depends on where he died. I doubt whether you'd get a car round the river side of the buildings without leaving obvious evidence. Anything with wheels needs investigating.' With difficulty, he refrained from adding, 'But of course you're aware of all that.' Serious crime teams knew their business; it was a sign of old age to need to dot too many i's. Instead, he said, 'I understand he was here with a golfing party. They'll need to be kept around.'

'I've already seen them. They're booked in for another two nights. They were ready to pack up and go home, but I told them we'd need them around for some time. I think they're going to stay on as booked.' Rushton as always was full of his own efficiency. Lambert, prepared to use it as usual, felt guilty that he should so resent the man's manner. Perhaps it was his fault: if there were more warmth between them, Rushton would not feel so continually obliged to demonstrate his own competence, like a newly appointed school prefect.

He said, 'If the place is so empty, perhaps we could clear one of the new residential sections completely for our use. I'll see the Manager.' It would not be too difficult: once the owners accepted the inevitability of a police presence, they would be ready enough to isolate it as far as possible from their own customers.

He looked across a gravelled courtyard to the picture window of what seemed to be a lounge. Anxious faces, male and female, stared back at him from behind the glass. Presumably the golfing party from which the dead man had

31

so abruptly departed. In spite of himself, his pulses quickened a little at the prospect of beginning his investigation among them.

'I'll go and see the Manager myself and arrange our set-up,' he said. It was as though he was deferring a pleasure until humdrum routine matters had been attended to. Already he had abandoned thoughts of a willing confession. People willing to proclaim their guilt came forward in those first emotional hours after the murder: the man out there had already been dead too long for that.

CHAPTER FIVE

In the hall of the old building, he took possession of the hotel register which was kept at the desk. It would be necessary to interview everyone who had been in the vicinity at the time of the murder: staff, guests, casual visitors who called for a drink and found themselves caught up in the potential drama and more usual tedium of a murder investigation.

Every movement would need to be checked, every story examined, every witness to innocent movements sought out. Elimination was the most usual form of progress in the early stages, slow but certain, focusing attention hopefully upon the two or three people with both opportunity and reason to kill. Except that it was rarely as tidy as that.

The Manager was young, harassed, thrown out of his stride by violent death, as more resilient men than he had been before him. Lambert found him on the phone to head office, absurdly anxious to reassure them that this affair was none of his making, that it could not have been foreseen. He assented dumbly to Lambert's arrangements for a Murder Room and the questioning of suspects, brightening a little at the thought that this business had a solution and his troubles might after all be finite. There were only four people staying in the newest red brick complex of rooms, which overlooked the eighteenth green. They agreed that the four should be moved to lodges at the other end of the development, so that the police could have the space and privacy they would need as the investigation developed and the evidence accumulated.

Lambert said, 'Thank you for your cooperation, Mr Clifford. I appreciate that these arrangements will mean a considerable amount of work, but I can assure you they are very necessary. The Scene of Crime team will disturb your guests much less this way.'

Clifford licked his lips and pulled at his tie. 'You think a crime was committed last night, then?' He was like a man who could not resist picking at a sore.

'Almost certainly a most serious crime.'

Lambert watched the young man sweating and wondered if it was merely his youth which he found irritating. 'Do you have a night porter on duty overnight?'

'Not at present. One has been appointed and will be here from the beginning of June. Of course we haven't been open very long and there are very few guests here at present. Ten days hence, we shall have the first of our large parties and—'

'So there was no one in charge of security in the small hours?'

'Not really. I live on the premises myself, of course, and I try to keep an eye on what is going on.' He looked at the wall behind Lambert, measuring everything in terms of the impact it might have at head office.

'And have you any idea what went on last night?'

'Not really. Mr Harrington's party stayed in the complex after they had eaten dinner in our restaurant. I could hear them—not that they were particularly noisy. And as I said, there are very few other guests to disturb at the moment. But with them being outside, the sound carries, and I could hear them in my flat, so that—'

'They were outside?' Lambert's sharpness made Clifford start. *Like a guilty thing upon a fearful summons,* the Superintendent thought, wishing immediately that such phrases would cease to spring unbidden to his mind.

'Yes.' The Manager looked like a man who regretted conceding so much.

When a CID man sees discomfort in a subject, his inclination is to investigate the cause. 'Where?'

Clifford clenched and unclenched his fists, quite unconsciously, it seemed. 'I think they were on the flat roof a couple of storeys above where they had dined.' He gave up the information reluctantly, like a man being made to talk about the weak area in a job application.

'You'd better show me.'

Clifford looked thoroughly miserable, but he nodded and stood up without a word. He led the way through a maze of corridors and staircases, where new extensions jostled against the more spacious proportions of the old house. They emerged suddenly into the bright sun and stood blinking at a view over the tops of tall trees to the river below them.

Lambert realized immediately why Clifford had been embarrassed that visitors should be up here. There was a row of four-feet-high steel posts set into the stone parapet around the edge of the flat roof. Between them, a single series of wooden planks ran horizontally, no more than fifteen inches from the floor level. Lambert walked over to examine two of the steel posts, confirming what was already obvious to both of them as he fingered the bolts at the top. 'Where are the other two levels of railing?'

Clifford tried to shrug the matter away, but managed only a rather ludicrous twitch. His too-vivid imagination projected him already into an investigation with the company safety officer. 'They're on order. The work should have been done by now. You know what builders are when the spring comes: they promise the earth to get the job, then when they have it you never see them. It was supposed to be part of our winter renovation programme: the old rails were removed because they were rotten.' He talked too quickly, as if hoping a multitude of detail would make a feeble explanation more convincing.

'So why were the public allowed access?' said Lambert wearily. He wanted to get on with the investigation, not persecute this unfortunate fall guy, but these were necessary preliminaries.

'They weren't.' Clifford went and looked outside the door they had just come through. He looked around for a moment and pounced upon a yellowing piece of card which lay face down on the carpet at the top of the stairs. He showed it without great hope to Lambert. Someone had scrawled in longhand with a green felt-tip, *'Roof not open to visitors.'* The card looked as though it had been lying on the carpet for some time.

Lambert forbore to tell the Manager that

the door to the roof should have been locked. They both knew that; no doubt if the Wye Castle had been fully staffed it would have been. Just as they knew that Clifford could have come up here and asked the party to leave the roof. If he hadn't been tired, and they hadn't seemed sensible, mature people. Lambert said, 'How long were they up here?'

'I couldn't be sure. Perhaps a couple of hours. My flat is some distance away, at the back of the main building. I didn't hear them after midnight, but I must have been asleep myself from about then.'

Lambert peered briefly over the edge of the roof, taking care not to touch that single, inadequate rail which marked its perimeter. Impossible to see anything from this height. He turned abruptly away and said, 'This door had better be locked immediately, and the key given to the Scene of Crime team in our operations room.'

He followed Clifford back through the passages, treading carefully through the gloom over ground which was familiar territory to the younger man ahead of him. When they had reached ground level, Clifford said jerkily, 'Will I be in trouble over that roof? The buck stops with me as manager, as usual.'

'Impossible for me to say, I'm afraid. It's not my department, but the coroner might have something to say.'

Clifford nodded abjectly, already seeing

37

unwelcome headlines. He was unlucky, of course. People like him took risks all the time with public safety, and for the most part got away with them. Lambert, suddenly sorry for him, said, 'Of course, if we are by then in the throes of a murder investigation, he might be excited enough to forget all about such things.' He was not sure whether he was trying to offer comfort or test the reactions of the manager to the idea of homicide within his dominion.

Clifford stopped so quickly that the Superintendent almost ran into him. 'You think this was murder?' The sickly glamour of the notion touched his face with a new animation. It was the first official acknowledgement of the idea that had both excited and dismayed him.

'It has to be a possibility. We should know by the end of the day.'

Back in the high hall outside, garish cherubs beamed down incongruously from the painted ceiling. The girl at the reception desk, who seemed to be enjoying the novelty of the situation much more than her boss, was waiting for Lambert to emerge from the Manager's office. 'There's a lady who insists on seeing you, Superintendent,' she said. It was part of her training to get titles right from the start.

Perhaps she saw the beginnings of his negative reaction: it was a conditioned reflex in him to suspect journalistic invasion wherever there was a whiff of sensation. She opened the door to a small ante-room before he could deny her and said, 'I put the lady in here.'

The woman who rose as he entered was tall and composed. Lambert, trained by long usage to make such assessments automatically, thought her about fifty. Her navy blue jacket and dress were severe, but becoming on her spare, erect figure. Her curls of grey hair were impeccably groomed. Only the hollows beneath the grey eyes gave any evidence of strain.

She said with the hint of a smile, 'I thought you might wish to see the widow immediately. I'm Marie Harrington.'

CHAPTER SIX

She put the emphasis on the second syllable, pronouncing the name as 'Maree'.

Perhaps that suggested the elegance which was Lambert's first impression of her. With his face composed to an appropriate solicitude, he wondered how near at hand was the WPC who should be dealing with this: the officer at the gate would never have directed the woman to him. He already felt at a disadvantage through coming later than he would have wished to an investigation already under way; he needed a distraught widow now like a hole in the head. Not a very tactful simile, he warned himself.

He stuttered, 'I'm sorry about all this . . . There was no need for you to rush here immediately, you know . . . Nothing you can do . . . They should have told you that.' Hearing his retreat behind the ubiquitous 'they', he felt both foolish and inadequate. He had dealt with this situation many times in the past; now he was thrown off balance by its unexpectedness, and annoyed with himself as a result.

Marie Harrington let him flounder through his explanations without interruption. The neat grey curls framed an intelligent face above a high, unlined neck. She said, 'The police came round at nine-thirty this morning. They said there was no need for me to do anything immediately, but I felt I must come. It's not much over a hundred miles, you know.' She was composed, perfectly organized in her thoughts and their expression. Absurdly, he felt that it was she who was helping him over the difficulties of the meeting, when the reverse should so obviously have been true.

'No. But there's nothing you can do here.' He looked round, as if expecting some kind of help or inspiration from the polished panelling. 'You should have been met by a woman constable—given a cup of tea and whatever information we can give you at this stage . . .'

'I came straight in here and went to the desk. None of your people was at fault: the men at the gate didn't direct me here.' She was smiling at him now.

He said stiffly, 'But you shouldn't be here, I'm afraid. Not at the moment.'

'I thought I had to identify the body. They told me that at home.'

'In due course. Not now.' He thought of the scene on the golf course, of the corpse being examined minutely for clues, treated as the thing it had become; of that thing being slid into a plastic bag and loaded without ceremony into the plain van. There was no place for a widow in that scene.

'I should prefer to identify Guy now, Superintendent. I promise you I shall not embarrass you.'

It was a moment to be firm but compassionate. He tried to muster the right expression. 'I'm afraid that is out of the question, Mrs Harrington. You must understand that after a death of this kind there are certain procedures—'

'A death of which kind, Superintendent?' He could have sworn she was gently mocking him, had that not been impossible in these circumstances.

'Mrs Harrington, I have to tell you that it does not seem at the moment that your husband died from natural causes—'

'Was he murdered?' She introduced the

word he had been carefully avoiding with a hint of impatience.

'That I cannot say. We are at the early stages of our investigation. But we cannot rule out foul play at the moment.' He was glad that Burgess was not here to witness his discomfiture, which was driving him into the very clichés the pathologist would have loved to hear.

Marie Harrington looked at him coolly for a moment. Her face was drawn, but the lines as her eyes creased a little were of humour rather than strain. 'So you think he was murdered.'

'I didn't say that. The Coroner has been informed of the facts. There will be a post-mortem examination. After that we may be able to tell you a little more about the circumstances of your husband's death.' He wished he knew exactly how much of those circumstances had been revealed by that faceless policeman in Surrey who had been charged with delivering the news of the death to the widow. He could not see a young constable being able to withhold much from this woman. He added rather desperately, 'That will be the time for you to identify your husband's body.'

'When he's been neatly sewn up and presented for viewing to the grieving relatives.' She smiled openly at him now, and he responded with a weak grin of his own; it seemed safer than speaking when he could think of nothing useful to mitigate the starkness of the picture she was painting.

She clasped her hands on her lap. She wore no nail varnish, and but one ring; it had a single large emerald, and was not on her wedding finger. She said, 'Mr Lambert, it might help things along a little if I tell you frankly that I shall not be grieving overmuch.'

It was delivered as dispassionately as if she had been announcing the time of a train. He had attended deaths before where he had suspected that spouses were not stricken with sorrow, but never one where a wife had so scorned to dissimulate.

'That is not my concern. Unless of course it is connected with the death.'

'Which it is not.'

'No. We shall need to have an account of your movements in the last few days in due course.' The human mind works so quickly that notions of a contract killing organized by this composed intruder flashed for a moment before him.

If he had intended his words to be any sort of threat to her, he would have been disappointed by her reaction. She said with scarcely a pause, 'That you are welcome to have whenever you want it. In the meantime, I may as well get on with the identification of his body.'

'As I have said, I regret that that is not possible at the present moment.'

'Why? That is what I have driven here to do.'

'I'm sorry about that. But there are certain procedures which cannot be overidden—'

'Mr Lambert, is there anything in law which demands that I identify my husband in a mortuary?'

He felt that she knew the answer to that as well as he did. 'No, but—'

'Is it not indeed in everyone's interest that this first formality is completed as quickly as possible?'

'I suppose so, but—'

'Then let us go out there and get it over with.'

He made a last attempt to protect her from what they would find. 'Please believe me, Mrs Harrington, when I say that I am not merely being awkward, or retreating behind police bureaucracy. Close relatives are invariably in shock after a sudden death, often more than they realize. It is for their sake, not ours, that we establish procedures to protect them.'

'In that case, let me go and identify my husband. I can assure you that it is for my own sake that I want to get this thing over. This is the end of one section of my life. I would prefer to see it terminated as soon as possible.' She was as calm as if she were arranging a shopping expedition or a business appointment.

He looked at her for a moment, then stood

up. He said, 'As you say, there is no regulation which prevents you from identifying the body now. As long as you understand that I advised you against it.' He moved towards the door, feeling even as he did so how churlish his surrender sounded.

Behind him, she said, 'I'll even sign a statement to that effect if you feel you need to be indemnified,' and he knew without looking that she was smiling at his awkwardness.

Lambert found an embarrassed WPC in the hall and sent her ahead to warn the people around the body of the widow's approach. Then he strolled slowly towards the spot himself, covertly studying the woman at his side as they went. Her heels were too high for walking over grass, but she moved carefully, without any serious loss of elegance. Under the bright sun, the small enclosure seemed in the distance innocent enough, but apprehensive faces peered at them over the screens as they approached.

The body had been sheathed in plastic and eased on to a stretcher; the van was standing with back doors open ready to receive it. Lambert said with a final nervousness, 'Are you sure you want to do this?'

The woman beside him did not even reply. She stood still to survey the scene for a moment, taking in the circle of anxious men, gathered around the static central figure as if awaiting some religious rite. Then she went

45

slowly forward, and the uniformed man at the head of the corpse drew back the plastic.

In the sudden, absolute silence, everyone heard the dry catch in Marie Harrington's throat and the uneven breathing which followed it; Lambert was curiously restored by this reassertion of the conventional. She recoiled involuntarily at what had been revealed, and he looked back to check on the presence of the WPC who had followed them discreetly from the old house.

But then the widow moved calmly forward, stood in straight-backed silence and studied the face below her. Lambert was glad to see that the head was laid so that the dark wound which blackened one side of it was downwards and almost concealed. Small residual patches of powder from the fingerprint officer dotted the blue wool on the corpse's shoulders.

She looked for a long moment, bidding farewell to the man who had been her husband: Lambert wondered in what terms that silent adieu was couched. Then she turned away from the corpse and looked the Superintendent full in the face. 'Thank you,' she said. 'That is my husband, Guy Harrington.'

Her face beneath the neatly coiffured grey hair had gone very white. Her hands at her sides trembled a little. She took a deep breath and set off towards the clubhouse. She was as erect as she had been throughout, but her shoulders now were stiffly held. Each of the circle around the body knew that she would not look back. In her unsuitable shoes, she shortened her steps, but moved quite steadily, as though she was unwilling to concede to the onlookers any sign that she was disturbed.

On the other side of the river, scarcely sixty yards away from them, a Jersey cow lifted its head and regarded them with huge brown eyes. It bellowed a long mournful moo, which echoed down the valley and emphasized the stillness of the place. As Lambert and the widow moved away, it stopped its chewing and stood motionless, staring with those timeless eyes, as if it comprehended this death, and its insignificance amid the cosmic scheme.

When they were about a hundred yards removed from the enclosure and the little tableau they had left was cautiously resuming movement, she said, 'Why the Sellotape on his clothing?'

'To pick up any hairs or clothing fibres from his killer,' said Lambert. It was the first time he had acknowledged openly to her in his own speech that he thought this a murder. 'The strips will be examined under a microscope in the lab and any suspicious material will be picked off for further investigation.'

'Do you know how he was killed?'

'Not yet. Perhaps by the end of the day we shall.' He did not tell her about the body being moved: to his relief she did not ask him about the blue-black blotching of the facial skin which had suggested the idea to them. He wondered anew whether she could be in some way involved in this death.

As if she read his thoughts, she said, 'Have you any idea yet who might have killed him?'

'If I had, I shouldn't be able to tell you.' They looked each other full in the face for the first time since they had left the ivy-clad hotel, and smiled. Perhaps they were both glad that the identification had been completed.

She looked at the ground, panting a little as they climbed the steep slope and skirted the eighteenth green. If she saw faces she knew peering at her covertly from the lounge in the residential block, she gave no sign of it. She said calmly, 'You may have deduced by now that I had no great love for my husband, Mr Lambert. You may as well know that I hated him. I don't feel as shocked by his death as you expected I should—perhaps I feel now that I've been half-expecting it for years.'

Lambert walked several yards on before he said, 'As I'm going to be in charge of what looks likely to be a murder inquiry, I should turn your question round upon you. Have you any idea who might have killed your husband?'

She picked a small wisp of dry grass from her severe navy skirt, studying it as though it affected her reply. They had reached the car park now. She stopped and turned to face him. 'I'm afraid I have no idea. But you have a wide

48

field. Guy had not many friends and a lot of enemies. I can think of many people who hated him enough to kill him.'

CHAPTER SEVEN

When Lambert made his first contact with the group of people with whom Harrington had spent his final evening, the widow's parting thought rang still in his brain.

The members of what had once been a relaxed holiday party were gathered in the lounge that had now become the centre of police operations. The death was still not officially confirmed as a homicide; in all essential respects it was being treated as one. The group which had assembled so happily for dinner some seventeen hours earlier carried signs of the tension now inevitable for them.

Once Lambert had introduced himself and Hook, an awkward silence fell upon them, as if each member looked to the others to make a move. It was Tony Nash who eventually said rather lamely, 'We were here on a golfing holiday, but none of us feels like playing now.'

'I can understand that,' said Lambert. 'Nevertheless, it would help our inquiries if you could remain here for a while.'

Nash looked sullen but uncertain. He glanced round the others, and Lambert divined that they had not concerted their thoughts and their opposition during the morning. He found that interesting. Now it was Meg Peters who said indignantly, 'That is out of the question!'

Sergeant Hook said in his best NCO manner, 'You are probably aware that we cannot require your presence here. Nevertheless, it would assist our work enormously. Obviously you had earmarked this time: the Manager tells us that you are booked in here for another two nights at least.'

'But surely you can see that circumstances have changed. There is nothing to keep us here now.' Miss Peters tossed her dark red hair imperiously and turned her green eyes full upon Bert Hook's. She did not like policemen, perhaps because they were rarely in a position to respond to her charms.

It was Lambert who said drily, 'Nothing except the good citizen's normal desire to see justice efficiently executed.'

If the woman was piqued to find the reply coming from a different quarter, she did not show it. She turned unhurriedly to the Superintendent, weighing the argument before she said, 'Now you're applying a little blackmail. If we wish to get on with our own concerns, we're accused of obstructing your inquiries. The next stage is to regard our exits as bringing suspicion on ourselves.'

Lambert assessed her. She sat with her head

turned slightly upwards, so that the strong nose jutted aggressively at him beneath a white brow that was furrowed with indignation. He said with a small smile, 'You assume, then, that this death was not accidental.'

It was said so lightly that they were left uncertain as to whether Meg Peters had fallen into some kind of trap. Eventually it was George Goodman who said, 'You will understand that we have been kept in the dark all morning about the death of our friend. Are we to assume he was murdered? No one has seen fit to tell us yet.'

'That is because we are not certain yet about the cause of death. All I can tell you is that we have been given reason to suspect foul play. Later in the day, when I have seen the pathologist again, I may be able to tell you more.' It was not easy to make the old bromides sound fresh, but most of them nodded as if they found his words reassuring. He thought that at the end of a long morning's wait they found any sort of information a minor comfort; the innocent ones, that is.

'May we ask what reason you have to suspect foul play?' Goodman was a JP. He knew enough of the law to be aware of his rights, enough of police procedure to know that he had little chance of a straight answer to his question. Unless, of course, it suited these men to give him one.

Lambert said, 'Forgive me, but you have all

been in touch with this business for rather longer than I have—I was in court for most of the morning.' He looked into the shrewd blue eyes of his questioner, searching his brain for Rushton's descriptions of the people in this key group. There was no mistaking the episcopal bearing of this man. 'You, I assume, are Mr Goodman. I understand you discovered Mr Harrington's body.'

'Yes. With Mr Nash here.' Goodman introduced Lambert and Hook to the other four members of the group. All of them, male and female, were aware as he did so that the man who would have taken this function upon himself yesterday had been violently removed from their midst. They did not resent Goodman's assumption of the role: they were glad indeed that someone had taken a general initiative in answering the police. Yet both of the women found his avuncular manner an irritation.

Lambert said, 'I've seen the spot where you found him. Did you think at the time that the death had a natural explanation?'

Goodman and Nash looked at each other. Each had assumed from the outset that someone had killed Harrington. For a moment they struggled with their own thoughts. Then Tony Nash said, 'There was a lot of dried blood on the side of his face.' He sounded like a schoolboy caught breaking the rules and trying to defend his action.

'Yes. Was the blood already dry and nearly black when you found him?' Lambert knew the answer; his interest was in the reactions of this group to the details of the death. There was a sudden, sick excitement in the air: he felt that the people around him realized that the murderer, if murder this was, was probably in this room. And as he took covert notice of the responses around him, he was aware of his own excitement too. The old adrenalin as the manhunt began: after twenty years he was still not sure whether it was a thing of shame or a necessary adjunct of his calling. Nash and Goodman were looking at each other again: though both knew the answer to Lambert's straightforward question, each seemed afraid of saying the wrong thing, as if a hasty word might incriminate him or others. It was a familiar first reaction to involvement in a murder investigation, but the Superintendent saw no reason to enlighten them about that. Creative tension, the social psychologist had called it at the last course his betters had thought it appropriate for him to attend. He was not sure whether to be gratified or dismayed by the discovery that what he had done instinctively over the years conformed with the latest theories of criminology.

Goodman said, 'It was almost black. He had been dead for some time.'

'Did you touch the corpse?'

Again the quick, confirmatory look at each

53

other. Then, not quite together, so that the effect was almost comic, 'No.'

'You had no idea, then, of the surface temperature of the body at the time?'

Goodman gave a little shudder and said, 'Look, Superintendent, is this really necessary? I imagine it must be very upsetting for the ladies in particular . . .'

Lambert looked round the five taut faces. He fancied that the two women were not altogether pleased to be distinguished as the weaker vessels in this way. 'Not strictly necessary, no. I am interested in why you should have assumed that your friend had not died naturally. Was there anything else about the body that struck you as odd?'

The other three were watching Nash and Goodman now with interest and expectation. There was no visible sign of the distress which Goodman had suggested they might be feeling. For the first time, Nash, brushing a strand of yellow hair clear of his right eye, spoke without an interrogatory glance at Goodman. 'Yes. He was lying—oddly.'

This time it was the two detectives who looked at each other, enjoying a little, not entirely innocent, collusion: they knew perfectly well what the man meant. Hook said, 'Oddly?'

'Yes. He was on his back, across the top of a mound. He could hardly have fallen like that, I think.' Nash seemed to have made this deduction only now, unless he was acting his puzzlement rather well. The audience was scrutinizing him closely.

Lambert said, 'Well, you may well be right.' He had no wish to communicate his own thoughts on the matter at this stage, though the image of that boxer splayed unconscious across the bottom rope of a ring came vividly back to him. The Welshman, Joe Erskine, he thought: the memories of adolescence were often more reliable than later ones.

'Let me put you in the picture about the way we plan to operate. I hope to know more of the details of this death before the day is out. If, as we all seem at the moment to be anticipating, Mr Harrington did not die from natural causes, we shall have to ascertain exactly how he did die. It goes without saying that as the people who were with him in his last hours, you will all be key witnesses in any investigation. Sergeant Hook and I will need to see you all individually in due course.'

'As murder suspects.' It was Alison Munro's first contribution since they had arrived. Sitting with long legs crossed in dark blue trews, she looked the most relaxed person in the room. Her dark eyes were quite impenetrable with the light behind her, but her wide mouth edged upwards with something very like mischief.

'Not necessarily. There are other explanations of unnatural death. Suicide, for instance, though I have to say I consider that unlikely in this case. Manslaughter, perhaps; though that might be a matter for lawyers to argue out rather than policemen.'

Alison toyed thoughtfully with a small gold ball-point pen, her slim fingers as elegant as its delicately tooled surface. 'Is there a possibility that anyone other than the people in this room was involved?'

'You're rather jumping the gun in your presumptions, Mrs Munro.' He noticed her little, involuntary start at the use of her name; possibly she recognized that the effort he had made to remember it signified her status as a suspect. 'But yes, of course the culprit you are presuming may be someone you don't even know. One of the things our team is busy with at the moment is checking exactly who was in the vicinity last night. Staff, visitors, anyone else who was in the area of the Wye Castle without good reason.' It was true, of course: it was the boring background to every investigation, which the media generally chose to ignore.

Secretly, he hoped this gathering contained his killer; moving out to the second and much wider range of suspects often meant crimes went unsolved. 'While I have you all together, let me ask you if there was anything you noticed last night which might be significant in relation to Mr Harrington's death.'

There was silence. A silence in which the

56

group looked at the carpet rather than each other. A significant silence, perhaps. He let it hang, and Hook knew him far too well by now to intervene.

It was the man in the room who was least at home with words who eventually found the silence unbearable. Sandy Munro said abruptly, speaking to his friends rather than the policemen, 'There was a bit of an argument at dinner.'

Lambert, professionally calm, apparently unaware of the looks of startled resentment at this unexpected disclosure, said, 'What sort of argument?'

'Well, almost a row, really.' Munro, having made the initial breach in their collective silence, looked miserably for someone else to complete the capitulation.

Meg Peters studied him calmly for a moment, her head slightly on one side, her remarkable red hair glinting in the strong light of the middle of the day. It was impossible to tell from her expression whether she was angry about his statement. Then she turned to Lambert and said, 'There was a little spat between Tony and Guy, that's all.'

Lambert said, 'Guy being Mr Harrington, I presume, and Tony—'

'Mr Nash.' There was a tinge of impatience in the words, edging the annoyance now evident in the set of her head.

Lambert, totally unruffled, studied her for a

moment before turning without haste to the youngest man in the room. 'What was the subject of this little disagreement, Mr Nash?'

'Nothing really, Superintendent.' Nash's smile was as ineffective as his words in dismissing the importance of the incident. He tried to shrug his broad shoulders free of the hunched tenseness which had beset them since his argument with the dead man had been mentioned. Then he looked round the room and found nothing to help him. The silence stretched; Lambert and Hook watched him steadily with expectant, interrogatory smiles. He said uncertainly, 'Guy said something about Meg to which I took exception, that's all. But he apologized and it was all forgotten before the evening was over.'

Lambert looked from Nash to the others, wondering if anyone was prepared to go further. Meg Peters met his eye arrogantly, parading her refusal to give him more detail like a badge of defiance. Goodman and Munro nodded, confirming Nash's low-key verdict on the episode.

It was Alison Munro who said, 'You must realize that the wine had been flowing fairly freely at the end of a day in the fresh air, Mr Lambert.' With her unforced smile framed by her sculpted dark hair, she was like an elder sister excusing boyish horseplay, and Lambert saw Nash resenting it even as she supported his dismissal of the row as trivial.

Lambert said, 'Well, if any of you thinks that there was a more lasting resentment, there will be ample opportunity for us to explore the matter together when I talk to you in a more private context. In the meantime, thank you for your cooperation.' He moved to the door, ignoring the fact that the cooperation he assumed had not yet been volunteered by the group. 'My advice to you is that you go on enjoying the golfing and other facilities of this place as fully as is possible in these distressing circumstances. I look forward to seeing each of you privately in due course.'

Sandy Munro wondered if he knew how much of a threat that sounded. He turned his thin face hard upon the carpet to conceal his relief as Lambert and Hook left the room. Even as he turned to the others to apologize for the small revelation he had made, he knew that he had concealed a greater knowledge from the police. And that others in the room had concealed things too.

And that one of them was his wife.

CHAPTER EIGHT

'Home for lunch. This almost amounts to dereliction of duty.' Christine came and stood at Lambert's shoulder as he sniffed at the first of the roses, a Climbing Ena Harkness on the south-facing wall outside the kitchen.

She was slim and alert, with dark, close-cut hair. In her tartan blouse and blue jeans, she looked trim and tidy even after a morning in the garden. She was almost a foot shorter than him as he smiled down at her and said, 'Home was on my way to the pathology lab.' He had more sense than to tell her that he had forgotten that she would be in the house rather than in school because of what he still thought of as the Whit holiday.

'A corpse, then. I have to be a detective myself to piece together what you're up to.'

'A killing at the Wye Castle. That new country club outside Hereford.'

'In pursuit of robbery?'

'Possibly. I don't think so. I'll know more when I've seen Burgess and get the results of his PM.'

'A light lunch, then.' She was amused always by his delicate stomach in the face of the pathologist's robust black humour. He watched her small hands making cheese and tomato sandwiches with what seemed to him amazing dexterity and speed. She did not like being watched, but had long since decided it was easier to endure it than to protest. She said instead, 'Is Bert Hook with you on the case?'

'He will be. We've hardly started yet. The body was found early this morning. By two of the suspects, apparently.'

'I saw Eleanor Hook last week at the parent-teachers evening. Young Kevin will be in my class next year.'

He recognized her resolute adherence to the world outside his work, which he now realized was one of her most valuable qualities. 'It seems no time since he was born.' Bert had married quite late and very happily. 'Old Bert will be forty-four now.'

'Very nearly as old as old John Lambert,' she said drily. 'Eleanor tells me he's started on an Open University degree.'

Lambert started to grin, then adjusted his features to neutrality just in time, as she slid the knife through the last sandwich and glanced sharply into his face. Patronizing the uneducated was the ultimate sin in Christine's short list. 'You mean old Bert's going to start answering back?'

'With any luck, yes. He might even start correcting your quotations: he's reading Humanities.'

Lambert, secretly delighted, pondered the implications of this new development for the CID double act that had baffled friend and foe alike over the years of their association. Hook's deadpan straightman had always concealed hidden depths; would he now begin to answer his chief's wilder literary sallies, or even, heaven forbid, offer his own initiatives in the area? Rank still had its privileges, which surely must be preserved, for the sake of discipline in the force.

He ate his sandwiches and considered the possibilities offered by a Barnardo's boy with a degree. It was material for D. H. Lawrence; but wasn't Lawrence on his way down again in the literary leagues of academia? He said to Christine, 'You'd enjoy rooting among the psyches of our main suspects at the Wye Castle. Pampered products of private education, to a man, I should think.'

Christine Lambert sturdily refused to contemplate the smaller classes and easier pastures of private schools. He was proud of her, immensely touched when, as often happened, people he came across paid unprompted tributes to her skills and persuasiveness as a teacher. He wondered why he should still find it so difficult to tell her so, why he preferred to tease her about her aspirations and her unstinting support of the underprivileged young. He saw enough of the results of deprivation to understand the importance of her work, even when she seemed sometimes to be swimming against an irresistible tide.

She watched him as he ate his sandwiches and scanned the newspaper headlines in their new conservatory. Scarcely half a stone heavier now as a grandfather than when she had first known him at twenty; greyer each year, lined increasingly about the eyes and mouth. She could not conceive of him doing anything other than the detection of serious crime. Once she had resented his single-mindedness, to the point where it had almost destroyed them as a pair; now she almost cosseted it.

She knew him well enough to know that even as he apparently relaxed with the sun on his face, his mind was busy already with the intricacies of his latest criminal puzzle. He left behind a cup still half full and a paper unopened.

Not for the first time, she wondered how such a man would endure retirement.

*   *   *

Lambert knew as soon as he saw Cyril Burgess that he was about to confirm murder. He had the bland smile, the annoying confidence of a magician who has performed a trick which is baffling to his audience but child's play to one with his knowledge and expertise.

'Do come through to the inner sanctum, John. You will not be disappointed, I think.' He indicated the way with an expansive gesture of an arm clad in dark blue worsted; with his Savile Row tailoring and silver-haired urbanity, he always suggested to Lambert the consultant surgeon he might have been.

Burgess took his visitor past his lugubrious, disapproving assistant, with Lambert trying not to speculate about the nature of the russet smears which marred the front of the young man's white overall. The Superintendent hoped he did not blench as he was taken to stand beside the body of the late Guy Harrington, almost as if the occupant of the slab was a patient who might be permitted visitors after a serious operation.

Lambert tried not to think about the huge incisions in the flesh beneath the sheet, but he had attended too many post-mortems to be in much doubt about them. Indeed, only his senior rank had enabled him to depute the police presence at this one to a hapless junior officer. He found this one of those occasions when the human brain and the human imagination refuse to remain inactive when commanded to.

Burgess brought out the notes he would later transform into an official report. 'Stomach contents,' he announced with relish.

'Tell me, please, don't show me,' said Lambert apprehensively: he knew that the information was necessary to establish the time of death.

Burgess grinned at the familiar effect his work was having on the Superintendent. 'A meal of steak, potatoes, calabrese and carrots, what appears to me to be sherry trifle, cheese and biscuits, was taken some time before death. Coffee, as usual, and a considerable quantity of alcohol—I'd say the best part of a bottle of wine, and perhaps five standard measures of spirits. Of course, the people at that meal had only to toddle to their rooms and fall into bed on the site—no need to bother about driving.'

Both of them knew the police could have found most of this from the people who had eaten and drunk with the dead man on the previous evening, but this was accurate and scientific—and the Coroner's Court would want to hear it. Lambert knew that Burgess liked to tease him by holding back the vital facts of his report as long as possible. He indulged him, in exchange for the unspoken assurance that he would not be asked to witness the internal organs of what lay before him beneath its sheet. 'Time of death?' he rapped, like one bringing an over-indulged child to heel.

'My dear John, you always want precision where precision is least possible.' Burgess pursed his lips, pretending to give careful consideration to a matter he had already decided for himself two hours earlier. 'The body temperature said our friend had been dead for probably not less than twelve hours when I got him here. From the digestive state of the stomach contents, I'd say the meal was completed not less than three and not more than five hours before death. I imagine that puts us some time after the witching hour?'

'Well after, I think. I understand they began what seems to have been a fairly leisurely meal at about eight. Probably they didn't complete it before nine-thirty.'

'Which would put death at somewhere between twelve-thirty and two a.m.' Burgess rubbed his hands with satisfaction. 'When all innocent citizens have entered the land of nod.

"Sleep that knits up the ravell'd sleave of care,
The death of each day's life, sore labour's bath,
Balm of hurt minds—" '

'Yes indeed!' Lambert interrupted ungraciously. Burgess, weaned on the detective fiction of the 'thirties, thought death ignoble if not accompanied by quotation. The CID man in Lambert made him add sourly, 'I doubt whether our killer at the Wye Castle will make himself so quickly obvious as the perpetrator of that Scottish bloodbath. I take it this *was* murder?' He gestured almost apologetically at the corpse between them.

'Oh, I think so.' The pathologist gave again his impression of the surgeon who has completed a neat and successful bit of work, but Lambert, an expert in Burgess-analysis, detected a faint whif of uncertainty.

'How did he die?'

'From multiple injuries.' Burgess made to draw back the sheet, but Lambert interposed firmly, holding it resolutely beneath the corpse's chin. He felt the cold through the

66

cotton. How quickly nature reduced a man to a carcase.

'He was hit with something?'

Burgess shook his head regretfully. 'Our old friend the blunt instrument? Not in this case, I fear. Though that might make the case too straightforward to be of real interest, of course.' He brightened as always at the thought of complexity in death.

'What, then?' Lambert was irritated as he had determined not to be by the conversational minuet he had to undertake to get information from this man without the lurid visual aid of a disembowelled corpse.

Burgess gave up his attempt to remove the sheet, like one capitulating to the whim of a wilful child. 'The injuries are commensurate with a fall from a height,' he said reluctantly. 'Depressed fracture of the skull, broken cervix, multiple internal damage and bleeding.'

Lambert breathed the long sigh of one who begins to see the way clearing at last. 'From an upper window?'

'Or a roof. On to a hard surface. Possibly concrete, but more likely compacted gravel: there are numerous fragments of stone in the wounds. Death was instantaneous.'

Lambert reviewed in his mind's eye the paths around the new residential blocks at the Wye Castle complex. They were paved. He said woodenly, as though feeding a cue to the main actor, 'But he wasn't found near a

67

building.'

'No. Hence the rather unattractive complexion.' Burgess nodded at the near-black patches on the face of the dead man. 'Which is repeated elsewhere on the front of the body. Mr Harrington had been lying face downwards for several hours after he died.' He made again to remove the sheet, and found himself once more resisted by the Superintendent.

'The body had been moved?' Lambert had deduced so much for himself in the hollow beneath the ancient beech where Harrington had been found, but he sought automatically the official medical confirmation of it.

'I'd stake my reputation on it,' said Burgess happily, as if reading the mind of a policeman who was mapping out his legal ground. 'But I couldn't say how he was moved. There were no marks on the body to indicate that.'

Lambert walked over to the neat pile of clothes that were waiting to be labelled. He stooped his tall frame over the brown brogue shoes that stood beyond the clothes, as if waiting to be resumed by the feet that would never don them again. They were highly polished brown brogues, without a trace of scuffing. 'He wasn't dragged from the scene of death to where we found him. It would show on the shoes in this dry weather.'

'Unless he was dragged by the feet,' said Burgess, reluctant to reduce the possibilities at this early stage. For a moment he relished the vision of a silhouette against the moon at dead of night, dragging his victim stealthily across gravel and fairway to deposit him in the deep shadow of the great tree. It had the melodrama of grand opera; it was Sparafucile in *Rigoletto.*

Then Lambert spoke and the vision faded. 'Surely not. There are no graze marks on the head either. Sorry, Cyril.' He rarely used the older man's Christian name: it was a respect for all men medical which had been bred into him in a working-class childhood, though he was scarcely conscious of it.

Burgess had known it was so really, for he had recorded in detail the state of the head, as of the rest of the corpse. The single large wound on the side of the head had been cleaned now, ready for viewing by distressed relatives; there were no other scratches upon the head or shoulders that would support his suggestion. He had merely allowed his taste for melodrama to overcome his sense of reality for a delicious moment. Somewhere within his sartorial rectitude, a trace of Dickens lurked. Balked of his sensational image, he tried his hand at detection. 'A strong man, then, to carry this. He weighs two hundred and six pounds.'

Lambert did a swift, automatic computation. Almost fifteen stone; at least Burgess had not gone metric on him yet. 'It would be nice to eliminate women and weaklings as easily as that. But he could have

69

been transported on something. The Scene of Crime team are examining the area in detail at this moment.'

Burgess looked cast down. 'Of course. A cart or something.'

'Almost anything with wheels. If it's still around, we'll find it, in time.' As he turned with relief away from the body, a thought occurred to him. 'Couldn't Harrington have simply fallen? You've just said he'd had quite a skinful.'

'He might, I suppose. Though I fancy that this man was well used to his booze, and it was taken over quite a long period, with lots of food. And if it was a simple accident, why on earth should someone move him afterwards?'

Lambert had already had that very thought. And another, more intriguing one. With the possibilities of accident or suicide still present, why had all Harrington's companions, the people who knew him well, assumed from the start that this was murder?

CHAPTER NINE

Alison Munro stepped from the shower, gathered the soft whiteness of the bath towel carefully about her shoulders, and moved into the bedroom. She flicked the untramelled black hair outside the towel with the swift,

70

unconscious gesture that had not changed over twenty years, a movement which remained unfailingly sensual simply because it was so undesigned for that effect.

Sandy Munro, sitting in an armchair by the double bed with its Laura Ashley bedspread, registered the gesture with a swift shaft of poignant desire for which he was unprepared. He continued to stare resolutely at his paperback thriller; he had not turned a page in over ten minutes.

An absurd pantomime began. He sat unnaturally still while his wife moved slowly about the room and began to dress. Each ostentatiously ignored the other's presence; each was acutely aware of the slightest nuance of gesture in the other.

He watched her in profile over the top of the pages he was not reading. As if in contempt of any hint of prudery, she turned wordlessly towards him as she dropped the towel and prepared to step into her clothes. Her flesh was firm still; only the tiny stretch marks of the pregnancies he had almost forgotten lined the white skin about her pelvis.

He tried hard to ignore what his senses were registering: his mind as usual refused to be so disciplined. Despite himself, he was acutely aware of the breasts, smooth and firm above the flat stomach, the long legs with the firmness about the thighs that came from years of controlling mettlesome horses, the dark bush between them that had filled him with such longing and excitement as a young man. With a startling rush of tenderness, he saw the small mole where her right leg met her pelvis, which even the tiniest bikini had always concealed, so that he thought of it as a symbol of their intimacy available only to him.

Or so he had always imagined: some devil now planted that thought in his mind. Even as he thrust it angrily away, he knew it would return.

When he spoke, it was as if the words burst out against his will, surprising him as well as her by their abruptness. 'We don't have secrets.' Four words only, yet still the unevenness of delivery was noticeable.

'Not normally, no.' The tension had built between them over their silence; she spoke quietly, trying to give the impression of control, but she did not trust herself with more than the single phrase.

'Then why now?' The words came harsh and quick, the monosyllables hammering at the roof of his mouth, the blood rushing to the roots of the hair she remembered as bright red in his youth, but which was now dulled with the first saltings of grey. She saw it and was moved, but the emotion caught at her tongue and made it even more difficult for her to speak.

Her lingerie was almost white, with the faintest green tinge which became apparent only as she moved into the darker part of the room; the delicate lace edging seemed designed to invite the caress he could not give as he sat nailed to his chair. She slid into the white linen dress with its squares and circles of dark green, shutting herself off from the vulnerability that had held him rigid, declaring herself inaccessible.

As she sat on the stool at the dressing-table, both hands went again to the back of her neck in that unconsciously sensuous gesture, checking that the hair fell loose and clear of her dress. Nowadays her hair was shorter and it was scarcely necessary, but he found its evocation of times past only the more moving for that. He felt a sense of hopelessness: normally when he felt uncertainty in any relationship, he turned to her for guidance. This time the darkness lay between the two of them, and she could not diffuse it for him.

He looked at her face in the mirror. To a stranger, it would have had its normal quiet, unaggressive beauty. The dark eyes above the high cheekbones were as wide and limpid as ever; the firm chin was set at its usual confident angle. Only the lips, thin and pale with strain, showed her consciousness of the question that lay between them. As he watched, their eyes met in the mirror. Her look in that instant had a mute, almost desperate appeal, a look so rare in her that it almost made him gasp. But he could not respond to what he recognized so clearly, and in an instant her eyes dropped and she picked up her hairbrush.

He watched the vigorous buffeting she gave to the lustrous cascade of hair at the neck, feeling with her the release that came with physical action, unable to find any such outlet for his own tension. He had not moved since she came into the room. Now he said as though the words were wrung from his lips by torture, 'I have to know.'

She did not look at him again in the mirror. She finished brushing her hair, put down the brush, and looked at it miserably for a moment. Then, almost imperceptibly, she shook her head, as if she were determining her own dilemma rather than answering the husband who sat so taut behind her.

The knock at the door made both of them start with shock, so immersed were they in their own contest of will and spirit. Then she whirled upon the stool and their eyes caught and held each other at last, wide with alarm at the interruption. In this at least he could take command. The external noise freed him at last from his rigidity; he felt the physical deliverance as he rose and went to the door.

'I'm afraid we need to ask you a few questions about last night. I trust it's convenient?' Lambert was at his most urbane, but he had the air of a man who would proceed with his business whether it was

74

convenient or not to his hearers. His head was barely clear of the lintel of the door, so that he seemed to tower over Munro, who now stepped back a pace as he glanced automatically at his wife.

The Superintendent was slim enough, despite his height, so that they could both see the rubicund presence of Detective-Sergeant Hook standing four square behind him. He should have been a reassuring figure as he followed his leader with cat-like Gilbertian tread into the room and shut the door carefully behind them. But with the unresolved tension lying between them, the Munros found the pair brought only menace into the room.

If Lambert sensed that he had interrupted something, he gave no sign as he went breezily into his standard patter. 'You are not legally obliged to say anything, of course, but the good citizen is normally only too anxious to assist in upholding the law.' He paused, wondering why Munro should be quite so put out by his presence: he must have expected to be questioned. Had these two been in the middle of a row? 'Perhaps I should tell you that it seems certain now that a serious crime has been committed.'

Munro licked his lips and hesitated. It was his wife who said, 'You're quite sure, then, that Guy was murdered?' This was ground they had already covered when he had met the golfing party together earlier in the day. She might have been just breaking the conversational ice, but he sensed she was temporizing, playing for a little time while she organized her thoughts.

'That will be a decision for the Coroner's Court in due course, Mrs Munro. But yes, our pathologist seems reasonably sure from his examination that Mr Harrington did not die from natural causes. Whether the death was a result of suicide, manslaughter or murder remains to be seen.'

'Or accident.' Sandy Munro found his voice at last—and discovered himself almost shouting. He said apologetically, 'Presumably Guy could simply have fallen to his death?'

He must have heard his wife's sharp intake of breath, for his head jerked towards her with a look of fear. In the long moment that Lambert allowed to stretch among them, the Scotsman still did not seem to grasp the mistake he had made. It was Hook who said eventually, 'You think that's how he died then, Mr Munro? A fall?'

'But surely you told us earlier in the day that he had fallen from the roof garden of the hotel during the night. I'm sure you did.' Bluster was not the right response, and Munro was in any case not a natural blusterer.

Lambert said blandly, 'No sir, I did not. For the simple reason that I was then not sure of the cause of death myself. But it seems you are right. The pathologist confirms that the nature of the injuries, internal and external, indicates

76

a fall from some height. Possibly from the roof or an upper window of the hotel, as you mentioned. I should be interested to know how you divined that so efficiently.'

'I—I suppose I guessed it from the state of the body.' Munro looked as miserable as a schoolboy before the master who has caught him out in a lie.

'You saw the body then? I understood the corpse was discovered by Mr Nash and Mr Goodman.' Lambert looked interrogatively at Hook, who confirmed the fact like a man responding to a cue, without needing to consult his notes.

'They must have told me.' Under stress, Munro's Fifeshire accent was strong enough for his low words to be almost undistinguishable. 'That's right, I remember. Tony Nash told me at breakfast.'

Now his wife's impeccable English accent rang out in stark contrast, beautifully enunciated, falsely bright in the quiet room. 'We were discussing it before you arrived this morning, Superintendent—we had plenty of time together in the lounge. I think George Goodman thought that that is what had happened as well.' She managed to make her supportive words sound light and confident, but the smile with which she tried to support them was a mistake. She was no more of a coquette than her husband was a blusterer.

The first lies of the case. Or were they

merely the first ones Lambert had detected? His mind flashed for a moment to the enigmatic figure of the dead man's widow. He thought of the way the corpse had been lying in that curious hollow of the golf course when he had first seen it, with its stomach thrust awkwardly at the heavens. The only visible damage had been that great smear of blackening blood on the side of the head. His own first thought had been that death might have come from a bludgeoning: it had taken the expert examination of Cyril Burgess to correct his impression that this might have been a mortal wound.

It was unlikely that Nash and Goodman, coming upon the body unexpectedly in the early morning, would have made more accurate assumptions about the cause of death than he had. Unless, of course, one or both of them had an earlier involvement in this death than its mere discovery.

He thrust aside that unwelcome thought and said, 'I should like to interview you separately, if you have no objection.'

'Here?' Munro's head did not move, but his eyes flashed quickly to his wife with what looked like desperation. She did not respond.

'It doesn't have to be: anywhere private would do. But here would be as good as anywhere.' Aware that both the Munros were thrown off balance, he was anxious to continue questioning one of them at least before they

78

could recover equilibrium.

'Right. I'll make myself scarce and leave you to it.' Alison Munro spoke up decisively. She did not look at her husband, who flashed at her a swift look of apprehension before he cast his gaze upon the carpet. He did not look up again until she had gone; for her part, she left without once glancing at her husband, even from the door.

There was a second small pink armchair and the stool in front of the dressing-table that Alison had lately occupied. The detectives disposed themselves as comfortably as possible on these inappropriate supports, moving them so as to sit facing the patently unhappy man who sat beside the bed.

At a nod from his chief, Hook said, 'The procedure, Mr Munro, is that we take statements from all the people who were in the vicinity when the crime was committed. We compare them, checking where the accounts agree and disagree with each other. There may be nothing sinister about a discrepancy: sometimes people just recall things differently. It all builds up a picture of what happened for us.'

'Shouldn't you warn me that it may be used in evidence?' Munro managed an anaemic smile.

'If and when someone is charged, we shall warn them that what they say may constitute evidence. Other people may of course be called as witnesses, if we, or for that matter the defence, considers their testimony would be useful. That, unfortunately, is probably still a long way ahead. What I like to do initially is talk fairly informally to the people who seem most likely to throw some light upon a crime. Sergeant Hook will take some notes, which may later be amplified into a written statement, which you would sign if you thought it a proper record of what you had said.' Usually he outlined these things to put people at their ease; this time, without any change in his wording or intentions, he seemed to be increasing the pressure on the wiry figure with the thinning red hair who sat before him.

'What do you want to know?'

'Let's start with the obvious. Can you think of anyone with good reason to wish Mr Harrington dead?'

Munro looked at the floor for so long that Lambert thought he was not going to answer. Then he said, 'He wasna' popular.' The voice was low, the accent as thick as that of an ancient Scottish caddie. Only the intensity of the sentiment prevented the bathos it threatened.

Lambert said gently, 'You'll need to elaborate for us, I'm afraid. Don't forget we don't yet know any of the people involved.'

As he hoped, Munro assumed that the people involved meant the party who had dined with Harrington on the previous night.

'All of us had had our differences with him over the years.'

'Yet you were all here with him on a golfing holiday.'

Munro looked as if it was the first time that had struck him as odd. He seemed for a moment to be trying to solve that puzzle for himself. 'We're members of the same golf club in Surrey. Two or three of us arranged the holiday; Harrington joined in late. I think George Goodman invited him, but I'm not sure.' Lambert, as a golfer himself, could see the picture: it was often difficult to refuse someone who wanted to join an outing of this sort without offence or embarrassment. As if in response to his thought, Munro now added, 'I said most of us had some reason to dislike him. That doesn't mean I can see any of us killing him.'

'Yet for what it's worth, my view is that one of you probably did.' Lambert let him dwell for a moment on that thought. Hook, with time to study these preliminaries at leisure, thought once again that, beneath his highly civilized manner, his chief in pursuit of results was as ruthless as the roughest hard-swearing city copper. Lambert leaned back a little, openly studying his man as he said, 'What cause had you in particular to dislike him?'

Munro's bright blue eyes looked fiercely at the two impassive CID men for a moment. Then he said, 'I worked for him. I didn't approve of his methods.'

'In what way?'

Munro stared hard at the carpet, as though he might find there the words he was struggling to form. 'I didn't approve of the way he treated people.'

'And?' It was like trying to get information from a captured prisoner.

'I'm an engineer. In my own field, I know what I'm doing. He took my ideas and claimed the credit for himself. Two patents registered in his name are really mine, but he never even acknowledged it.'

'Anything else?'

Munro looked quickly into Lambert's face, then down again at the complex pattern of the carpet. He shook his head. 'That's all.' The sharp Scottish features set like marble. Whether or not that was indeed all, it was all they were going to get.

Lambert gave a scarcely perceptible nod to Hook, who flicked ostentatiously to a new page in his notebook and said, 'Will you tell us all you can remember about the events of last night, please, Mr Munro?'

'Beginning when?' Munro, licking dry lips, was plainly not looking forward to this. Lambert would have given a lot to know whether he was normally of a nervous disposition, as he now appeared to be.

'I understand all your party ate together. Let's begin with that meal, unless you think

82

there is anything earlier in the day that might be significant.'

Munro shook his head and appeared to relax a little. 'It was a normal enough meal. It was spread over quite a long time. There were four courses and coffee, and we didn't hurry over them.'

'And quite a lot was drunk, I imagine.'

Munro looked at him sharply, trying to work out whether any criticism was implied in the remark. 'Aye. Some had more than others.'

'Yes. Mr Harrington for one, according to the post-mortem.'

Munro looked shocked; whether by the extent of their knowledge or by Lambert's unabashed revelation of it, it was impossible to tell. 'He could take it. He was well used to it.' For the merest instant, the disapproval bred by those formative years he thought he had left for ever in the shadow of the manse was evident in his contempt.

'You would not have said he was drunk, then?' Munro began a small, uncooperative shrug, but before he had completed it Lambert had rapped at him, 'This looks like a murder inquiry: I should prefer it if you were as accurate as possible.'

'Guy could take his drink. Sometimes he used the fact that other people couldn't.'

'Times like last night?'

'No.' The negative came almost too quickly, as though he already regretted his indiscretion.

'Guy drank quite a lot, but he was in good form for most of the evening.'

Lambert wondered whether the Scotsman was just uneasy with words, or whether he was deliberately leading them into an area of revelation. Perhaps it was a little of each; he seemed almost unconsciously to be accepting that he had something of interest to tell them.

'Just for most of it?'

'There was the row—a disagreement anyway—during the meal.'

'Between whom?'

'Between Guy and Tony Nash.'

'About what?' It was like drawing teeth, but Lambert was well used to that by now. He had heard about this dispute when they first met the group earlier in the day, but it was interesting that Munro seemed drawn back to it now.

'I'm not quite sure. I don't think many of us were at the time. Tony just flared up at Guy. I'm not sure what Guy had said, but when Tony shouted at him he insisted that he had only been joking.'

'And do you think he was?'

For the first time since the detectives had entered the room, Munro smiled. It was a wry mirth, but a hint that he could laugh at himself. 'From what I said earlier, you could hardly consider me an unbiased witness. But no, from what I know of the two of them, I would have thought that what Guy said was

84

quite malicious, though he shrugged it off as though Tony was being absurd.'

'What exactly *did* he say?'

'I don't know. I suspect no one did, except the two of them. We were all busy with our own conversations when we heard Tony shouting.'

Hook looked up from his notebook. 'Are you telling us you've no idea what the dispute was about?' His tone was quite neutral, yet he managed to imply that the suggestion was absurd.

It had the desired effect. Munro speculated where he had not intended to. 'I think it might have had something to do with Meg Peters. I couldn't be sure.'

Lambert pictured the youngest of the group: with her green eyes and red hair, she was not easily forgotten. Sex and money, in that order, were the primary elements in murder cases. It was statistics, not chauvinism, which made him consider the striking Ms Peters might be at the heart of this one. It was certainly something to be investigated in the interviews to come. He said, 'At what point in the meal did this incident take place?'

'I think we'd just got our dessert.'

'So a good deal had already been drunk. By those who were drinking, that is.' If he was teasing Munro, his face, grave beneath the plentiful iron-grey hair, gave no acknowledgement of it.

85

'I suppose so. We'd had plenty of wine with the meal. Tony likes a glass or two, and you say you know about Harrington. But we'd eaten quite a big meal with it. No one was drunk.'

'What time did the party break up for the night?'

Munro must have expected they would come to this, but they both saw him stiffen uneasily. 'I'm not absolutely sure. We sat out on the flat roof for quite a time chatting after we'd finished eating. It was a wonderful night.' The phrase suddenly struck him as inappropriate, but he found the officers quite impassive when he glanced at them in nervous embarrassment. 'I suppose it must have been after midnight when we broke up.'

'And you went straight back to your room?'

Munro's hesitation made his reply more pregnant than it would have been without it. 'No. I went for a walk. I felt I needed it before I could sleep.'

'I see. Were you accompanied on this expedition?'

'No. I didn't go far. Just down to the gates of the estate.'

Lambert did a swift calculation. About a mile and a half in all. Half an hour: more if he deviated from this route. Ample time to commit a murder and move a body. 'Did you stick to the road?'

'Mostly. I strolled out to the green nearest to the gates—the sixth, I think. It was a beautiful moonlit night.'

Not a braw one: Lambert was glad to avoid the Caledonian cliché, which he fancied would now be confined to stage Scotsmen. 'Can anyone vouch for your whereabouts at this time?'

Munro swallowed. 'No, I don't think so.'

'Your wife didn't accompany you?'

'No. She'd had a tiring day. It was late for her already. She likes to get to her bed early.'

For the taciturn Scot, it was a positive welter of explanation. Lambert wondered if it had any significance, or whether the man was merely anticipating with relief the end of the interview, as witnesses often did. He had to remind himself that the innocent as well as the guilty could find these exchanges an ordeal. He said, 'Was she asleep when you got back to your room?'

Munro swallowed, contemplating the carpet again, as if his record of the previous night's events was written there and he was checking it. 'Nearly, I think. We didn't speak again.'

They paused; the only sound in the room for a moment was the tiny scratching of Hook's ballpoint. Then Lambert said, 'You've already told us you thought Mr Harrington fell to his death from the roof or a window. Did you hear anything after you got back that might support such a view of the death?'

'No. I was asleep very quickly.'

They let him go then, with the usual

87

admonitions to come back to them immediately if anything occurred to him subsequently which might have a bearing upon the case. He nodded earnestly and was gone.

Lambert was left wondering why such a transparently decent man should tell him so many lies.

CHAPTER TEN

The tension of a murder inquiry, which can be disguised but never eliminated by surface politenesses, makes one forget one's surroundings. When the two large men left the small room which was the temporary home of the Munros, they were surprised to find the day outside as serene and innocent as ever. And it was evening: Hook checked his watch with surprise and found that it was almost seven. 'Call it a day?' he said hopefully.

'After we've seen Mrs Munro,' said Lambert. 'I'm anxious to get to her before her husband does, if we can.' He strode determinedly down a passage towards the area they had established as a temporary centre of operations. Hook followed resignedly, but without any real resentment: he was not yet so inured to CID routine that his adrenalin level failed to rise with the development of the hunt.

'I suppose you're anxious to be away to your

studies,' Lambert called over his shoulder as he skipped nimbly down a staircase. It was the first indication Hook had had that the Superintendent was aware of his Open University venture, though he had known the discovery was inevitable. In truth, he had merely been hoping to get home before his boys disappeared to bed, but he said, 'I find it easier to work at the other end of the day. Some of the television programmes are put out early in the morning, as well.'

'What literature are you studying?'

Typical of the chief to consider that any sensible man would be studying literature, thought Hook. Perhaps he would choose Sociology as a second-level course, just to annoy Lambert. 'There isn't very much on the Humanities Foundation Course. I've been reading *Hamlet*; that comes up soon.' He panted along behind the taller man, who seemed determined to keep just in front of him even though the path now allowed room for them to walk alongside each other.

'So you're wishing some of that "too solid flesh would melt, thaw and resolve itself into a dew"!' said Lambert with satisfaction, as he finally allowed the substantial figure of his sergeant to draw alongside him.

Hook drew in his paunch with dignity. 'You don't think "sullied" might be a more correct reading?' he asked calmly. He walked ahead of his chief towards the murder room, resisting the temptation to turn and check whether his jaw had really dropped in astonishment. There might be ancillary benefits to this study business which he had not even considered when he embarked upon it.

In the group of lodges which had been cleared of visitors, the lounge was already looking like a murder room. The filing cabinets and telephones were installed, the fingerprint crew were recording their findings at a table on the far side of the room, a WPC was compiling lists on one of the now ubiquitous word-processors. The number of plastic bags containing materials which might eventually constitute evidence was growing at its usual surprising pace. Detective-Inspector Rushton, hearing their voices in the corridor, was on his feet by the time they entered the room, stepping forward like a Head Waiter welcoming patrons to his domain.

'Ah, Mr Lambert, we couldn't find you anywhere. I thought you must have gone.' He managed to make their absence sound like a dereliction of duty, though in truth he was probably only emphasizing his own industry and orthodoxy. Rushton, to be sure, would have made sure the rest of the team knew exactly what he was about and where he had gone if he had disappeared to interview Munro; Hook was glad to note that Lambert did not immediately tell him where they had been.

'Where's Mrs Munro?' was all he said.

'I think I saw her in the main hotel just now. She was talking to George Goodman.' Rushton was a pain in various parts of the anatomy, according to taste, but he was undeniably efficient.

'Would you tell her I should like to see her here right away, please?' Lambert went without waiting for acknowledgement into the inner office they had already assigned as an interview room. It was normally a staff rest-room. They had found a desk and a swivel chair for him, but magazines had been stacked hastily on a coffee table in one corner. In another, a small washbasin received the water dripping from a leaky tap. Above it, the mirror-fronted door of a medicine cabinet hung slightly open, revealing the bottles of paracetamol and plasters which might be necessary for the day's minor ailments. He had a sudden image of a doctor's consulting-room. Perhaps it was not inappropriate, though his investigations would be mental rather than physical.

Alison Munro was with him within two minutes. Rushton came briefly into the room with her, but the impression was that she dismissed him at the door rather than that he left tactfully when his role as usher was complete. This woman moved with a grace and poise which was the more telling for being effortless and unconscious. She composed herself elegantly into the armchair Bert Hook had positioned for her; the Sergeant was left wrestling with the word 'breeding', a concept which his Barnardo-boy background sternly resisted.

Even Lambert was thrown into an opening which sounded almost apologetic. 'Thank you for coming across here so promptly. All this must be rather distressing for you.'

She weighed the cliché carefully, then underlined its feebleness by responding seriously, 'No, I don't think so. I think I might find the mechanics of a murder investigation quite interesting: it will certainly be a new experience. And I felt shock rather than distress when I heard of Guy's death.'

Her eyes, set so deeply that they looked almost black, looked steadily at Lambert, estimating his mettle, wondering whether he would take up the challenge. He merely nodded, looked thoughtfully at his nails, and said, 'Why do you think your husband assumed that Mr Harrington had been killed by a fall, Mrs Munro?'

If she thought the contest had been joined, she gave no sign other than a slight easing forward on her chair. She had been prepared for this, even if she had expected to be led to it more gently. 'Sandy is an intelligent man, Superintendent. Probably he deduced it from what the others told him about the appearance of the body. And from what you told us earlier, it seems to have been a reasonable deduction.'

'Perhaps for someone who had all the facts. Your husband had apparently not even seen the body himself.' He was sure she stiffened a little at his use of the word 'apparently'; whether the reaction stemmed from fear or merely from annoyance at the implied slur on her husband's probity he could not be sure. 'I inspected the body in the place where it was found. I have seen many deaths, Mrs Munro, but I did not think at first that this one had been the result of a fall. It took the specialist knowledge of a pathologist to tell me that.'

She looked full into his face, as she had done throughout the exchange. 'I am sure Sandy would not claim more expertise in these things than a man of your experience, Mr Lambert.' She allowed herself a small, ironic smile, which stopped well short of contempt. Lambert, who had considerable experience of the breed, was reminded of the defence barrister who, presented with an item which damages his case, maintains an outward calm at all costs whilst his brain furiously reorganizes strategy.

As if she was aware of his comparison, she stroked the hair she had washed just before he appeared, like a counsel checking her wig. But her impeccably fitting helmet of black hair was no archaic prop of authority. She said coolly, 'I would remind you again that my husband has spoken to the people who actually found the body. You can imagine that the matter was almost the sole topic of conversation among our group this morning. He may well have picked up information or impressions from the people who had seen more than he.'

It was a fair point, and one precisely made: again he could see her in a courtroom context. He had already considered her argument. Almost certainly one person at least among this group knew exactly how Harrington had died. That person could have communicated the knowledge to others, whether unwittingly or for some other, as yet undefined, purpose. He said, 'Of course you are right. That is certainly one possibility.'

The small, firm chin jutted forward half an inch towards him. 'If you think there are others, you should take it up with Sandy, Superintendent.' It was the first time she had used his rank, and she contrived to make it sound an insult. This calm woman with her well-organized defences was not going to be easily caught out; for the present, he was ready to accept her dismissal of the matter.

'I have already talked to him about it, Mrs Munro. And we may return to the matter in due course.' This time he was sure she was disconcerted: perhaps she recognized his tactic of interviewing her before she could confer with her husband about what he had said to them. 'What we need from you at this point is an account of what you remember of last night.'

He had deliberately left his terminology vague, in the hope that she might feel threatened. She acknowledged the ploy only by correcting it. 'Last evening, you mean, presumably. I was asleep for most of the night.'

It was Lambert's turn to smile and score a point. 'Presumably most people I see are going to tell me that. Including one or more who spent a portion of the night murdering Mr Harrington.' She conceded the point with an answering smile: had he been expecting to chill her with the argument, he would have been disappointed. 'Would you give me your account of events, please, from the moment when your party got together?'

She paused, organizing her thoughts, deciding, he was sure, what to tell him and how to phrase it. 'We had a drink before we went into the meal. Everyone was pretty light-hearted. The men were twitting each other about the afternoon's golf. I think Meg—Miss Peters—found it irritating. I can understand that: there's nothing more irritating than other people's golf, especially if you don't play yourself, as she doesn't. And we'd had a tiring day.'

'You had been out with Miss Peters during the day?'

'Yes; sightseeing and shopping: I don't know which was more tiring. Anyway, we were

95

certainly ready for the meal.'

'And did anything untowards happen during that?'

Again she gave him that slightly scornful smile, as if disappointed in an adversary who could be so transparent. 'You have heard of the little spat between Tony Nash and Guy. I'm not sure I can add anything to enlighten you.'

'Try, please. If it has nothing to do with this death, no one will suffer.'

She did not comment on whether it might or might not have a connection. 'Tony took exception to something Guy said, that was all. I didn't catch what it was, but I've no doubt it was a remark about Meg's affections.'

'Miss Peters is here with Mr Nash. I am right in assuming they are having an affair?'

She frowned a little, looking for once away from him. Her dark eyelashes blinked with concentration; he had not realized until then how long they were. 'I suppose so. That word covers such a multitude of relationships nowadays. I think they intend something more long-term than I would understand by the word. But I suppose you will ask them about that in due course.'

'If it seems likely to have any bearing on this case, I probably shall, yes.'

She nodded, looking for the first time at Bert Hook, studiously recording her replies in his notebook. 'Guy had dallied a little himself

96

with Meg. I've no doubt that gave an edge to his comment. And to Tony's reaction, for that matter.' She had an air of ennui at the tiresomeness of men in these matters, but he had little doubt that her analysis of the incident was a shrewd one.

'Mr Nash's reaction was not what you would have expected?'

Again she paused, weighing her reply like an expert witness. 'Tony had worked for Guy for years. Harrington did not expect his workers to speak out of turn. I had never heard Tony do so before.' There was a little contempt here, which she didn't trouble to disguise, but it was not clear whether it was for the employer's exploitation of his position of power or the employee's craven acceptance of it.

'Did you hear what was said?'

'Not the bit that gave offence. The first most of us heard was Tony Nash shouting, "Either you take that back immediately or you'll be sorry!" I remember the exact words because they seemed to come straight out of a B movie. But Tony was serious enough about it.'

'And how did Harrington react?'

'Oh, he laughed it off. But he was shaken.' She said it with relish, then looked annoyed that she had revealed so much of herself. 'Things were smoothed over and the meal went on without any further disagreement. No doubt the wine helped.' This time she was carefully and successfully neutral: he could not tell whether she applauded the emollient effects of the grape or deplored its capacity to blunt reality. Probably neither.

She was a woman whose insights and judgements would be worth sharing—always assuming that she was not involved in the crime. He said, 'Did you see anything during the evening which would indicate in the light of what happened later that one of your party wished to kill Mr Harrington?'

He half-expected her to dismiss the notion with the view that that was his business rather than hers, but she did not. The pale brow beneath the dark hair wrinkled a little, the strong, small hands clasped for a moment in front of her. Then she said, 'No. Apart from the incident we've just discussed, no one seemed particularly overwrought.' She seemed as though she would genuinely have liked to offer them something they might use. It made Lambert wonder how good an actress she was.

'I must ask you whether you know of anyone with a reason to kill Mr Harrington. Needless to say, your reply will be treated in the strictest confidence.'

She looked at him with a cool smile; she seemed to be genuinely enjoying the question and the suggestion that she might have such knowledge. Lambert remembered the intensity of her husband's reaction to the same inquiry.

They could scarcely be a more different pair, in temperament and background. Yet his guess was that they would be fiercely supportive of each other: perhaps the old idea of the attraction of opposites had something in it, or perhaps the differences one saw clearest were the superficial ones, disguising the more important similarities of philosophy and outlook that lay beneath.

She said, 'Guy Harrington excited strong passions in people, Mr Lambert. With your extensive experience, I'm sure you have found they often prompt people to violence.'

She was taunting him a little, throwing back his earlier suggestion about the benefits of experience. Trying not to be nettled, he said evenly, 'As a generalization, that would be correct. Can you be rather more specific about the people involved here?'

She crossed her legs; Bert Hook persuaded himself that he was admiring only the rich maroon leather of the high-heeled shoes below the nylon. 'I doubt whether I can help you much there: I don't know any of them particularly well. Meg Peters had certainly known Harrington well in the past. I don't know exactly how well, but no doubt the efficient machine that is the CID will soon discover that. Tony Nash was certainly more upset than I have ever seen him last night. George Goodman had known Harrington for a very long time: whether there is anything of great moment in their pasts I have no idea. George seems far too avuncular to perpetrate homicide, but I suppose under stress the unlikeliest people are capable of foolish actions.'

It was the very admonition Lambert found himself giving frequently to people drawn into investigations; he found it curiously disconcerting to have it thrown back at him. He noticed how the golfing party had suddenly become 'them' rather than 'us'. Perhaps it was natural that she should regard herself and her husband as being above suspicion. He said gruffly, 'I should like you to give us now an account of your own movements after the party broke up at the end of the evening.'

Suddenly and unexpectedly, she was on edge. She must surely have expected this, but it had made her nervous for the first time. 'We sat together on the roof of this building for quite a long time after the meal was over. I had a brandy: someone was passing round a half-bottle—Guy, I think. It was a beautiful, moonlit night, as you may remember. It was still quite warm at around midnight. It must have been quite late when we broke up; I wasn't wearing a watch, so I couldn't be sure of the time.'

She was talking quickly, rushing on inconsequentially, postponing the moment she knew was inevitable. Lambert said, 'And where did you go yourself at that point?'

100

'Well, I wandered round for a little while before going to bed. Perhaps we'd all drunk a little too much.'

Lambert doubted if that was true in her case. He said, 'I believe your husband went for a walk on his own. You chose not to go with him?'

She flashed him a look of fierce suspicion, as if she thought he was trying to trap her. Then she relaxed; but it was a conscious effort. He could see her working at it, like someone concentrating on releasing muscle tension at the beginning of a yoga class. She said 'No. I didn't want to be with Sandy then. I felt rather—confused. I suppose when I think about it now that I really had had a little too much to drink.' Her little giggle sounded as false in her own ears as it did to the men studying her. It could have been explained as simple embarrassment, but she had shown no previous signs of being easily discomposed by the confession of a social peccadillo.

'Where did you go, Mrs Munro?'

The simple question became suddenly important, the atmosphere highly charged. Probably it was because they all recognized at the same moment that a woman who was not normally evasive, who perhaps even scorned to be so, was trying to disguise the truth. Alison Munro brushed a tress of dark hair impatiently back from her cheek, as though it had let her down by coming adrift at this point. She said, 'I

101

really don't remember, Superintendent Lambert. I shouldn't like Sergeant Hook to record what wasn't true.' It was a brave attempt at her former ironies, but no more than that.

Lambert said quietly, 'So you are saying that you cannot account for your movements at the time when Guy Harrington was very probably being killed.'

'Guy was not killed during that period, Mr Lambert.' She spoke with such conviction that she startled the two experienced men. 'For what it's worth, I didn't go far. I think I wandered around the outside of the old house and then along the paths among the newer building blocks before I went back to our room.'

'Did anyone see you? You can understand, I am sure, that we should like to have your movements confirmed.'

'I'm afraid not.' The reply came too promptly from someone who should have been looking for corroboration of her story; perhaps she knew that such confirmation was not possible.

Lambert, who had already decided he did not believe her, pressed as hard as he dared with a witness who was still a citizen voluntarily helping the police to pursue their inquiries. He said, 'So you did not speak to anyone in this period between when the group broke up and you returned to your room?'

'No.' Again the reply came so hard on the heels of his question that there was scarcely a pause between. Then she said more deliberately, 'If I had done, he'd be able to confirm my story, wouldn't he?'

Lambert wondered if there was anything to be deduced from the fact that she should assume it would be a male she might have met. She had a point, of course: he was going to check with the others in her party, so that if she had met one of them it should come out in due course. Unless both of them wished to conceal it. He said, 'Did you speak with your husband when you got back to your room?'

The dark eyes bored into his, the striking features which framed them seeming paler than ever. He was professionally inscrutable, exuding a calm he did not feel. Alison Munro said, 'No, I don't think so. Sandy was in bed and probably asleep. He gets off very quickly.'

She looked down at the fraying edge of the carpet to her right, desperately wishing that she had been able to compare notes with her husband before this meeting.

She was sure already that she had made the wrong reply to this last, crucial question.

WEDNESDAY

CHAPTER ELEVEN

'Any news from Jacqui?' John Lambert was pleased to get his question in before Christine could inform him. Usually when he was on a case he forgot even his favourite daughter.

'Not a lot. She saw the gynecologist yesterday. The baby had turned himself over again and they put that right. Otherwise, everything is as it should be. About a fortnight, they think.'

As he had anticipated, she was absurdly pleased that he had asked without being prompted; he felt a shaft of guilt that his omissions should be so manifest. Yet he cared deeply about the progress of Jacqui's pregnancy. It was the old wall he erected between work and home. Other people, even other policemen, managed things better. He was well aware how he had almost broken their marriage twenty years earlier: neither he nor Christine ever spoke of those days now. The stubborn, stone-faced young Inspector and the lonely woman who had shrilled her resentment at him might have been two other people, removed now from their lives.

'You'll make a good grandfather, once you've got used to the idea again.' As usual, she sensed his difficulty. He felt despite the grey hairs and crows' feet he saw in the bathroom mirror each morning that he was still at the height of his powers. It seemed no time at all since he had held seven-year-old Jacqui and her sister upon his knee to watch the television serials at Sunday tea-times. Last year Caroline had made him a grandfather; now Jacqueline was about to do so again.

He wondered if there were children involved in the death at the Wye Castle. None had surfaced yet, but people were capable of violent and irrational actions where their children were involved. He had seen such passions often enough in his work; he felt more in himself than he cared to acknowledge of that primitive, disturbing extremism which could strike at a man pursuing the interests of his children.

He picked up Bert Hook on his way to the murder room at the Wye Castle; the Sergeant lived in a village which could be included on a route to the hotel by using some of the myriad lanes of the area. The big car had to run slowly for a mile or so behind a farm tractor, on a road where packs of wool had plodded six centuries earlier at the direction of the first British capitalists.

Was their victim a descendant of that entrepreneurial line which began with the Cistercians in their monasteries? It was a depressing thought: from what they had learned already from his wife and friends, Guy Harrington seemed a markedly less benevolent operator of economic power than those monks who had filled the valleys with sheep and sucked in the gold of Europe to pay for their wool. The exploitation of capital seemed to have a very different philosophical basis in the nineteen-nineties.

The tractor turned at last into a field and Lambert moved thankfully out of second gear. He broke the silence that had prevailed between the two big men since their initial greetings with 'Any ideas yet about a murderer?'

'None whatsoever,' said Hook, so promptly that he must have been anticipating the question. Then, as if he thought this cheerful denial unbecoming in one of his profession, he said, 'The Munroes are trying to hide something, but whether it's murder or not I wouldn't be sure.' He glanced sideways at his chief, but found as he expected that there were to be no great revelations from him at this stage.

'The key thing is obviously what happened in the two hours after the group broke up. Both Munros have already lied to us about that—how extensively remains to be seen. I wonder which one of them really returned to their room first.'

'Alison Munro didn't seem to me a woman who would lie habitually.' Hook stared steadily away from Lambert and through his side window at a cloud of starlings wheeling round an ineffective scarecrow: he had been ridiculed too often in the past for his susceptibility to dark eyes and soft contours.

Lambert gave a sideways glance of amusement at the profile so resolutely turned towards the fields. 'But she is married, Bert. Remember, "Though women are angels, yet wedlock's the devil." Marriage can make a liar out of an honest woman.'

Hook tried not to look triumphant: he had identified the source of the Superintendent's quotation, for Lambert had used it on him before. He said calmly, 'I don't think Byron can claim to be the best authority on wedlock.' The starlings twittered a celebratory chorus for his coup as they passed within thirty yards of them; he wound his window right down to allow them maximum effect.

'If the Open University is going to remove all sense of decorum, I shall have you transferred,' said Lambert indignantly. 'You'll be correcting my little gems next.'

'Isn't it Byron who speaks of the critic who had "just enough of learning to misquote"?' said Hook. This time he could not contain his smile, which broke in full glory over his rubicund features. Wedlock, despite his chief's view, was a most useful institution; was it not his wife who had directed him to the book reviews in the *Observer*, whence he had quarried this useful nugget?

There was less evidence of melodrama at the Wye Castle Hotel and Leisure Complex than on the previous day. The manager watched their arrival with anxious eyes, then went back to hopping nervously among staff who, like him, had too little to do in the absence of new guests. Outside the lodges which housed the murder room, there was but a single white police vehicle announcing its presence. But the CID men, levering themselves out of Lambert's ageing Vauxhall, recognized several unmarked vehicles which belonged to their team.

The clouds were high, but they raced on a brisk breeze above the ivy-clad crenellations. They walked beneath the high wall whence Guy Harrington had fallen to his death. Lambert was not sure whether he wished to tune his mind to detection by visiting the spot where he was sure Harrington had died, or whether he merely wished to savour the view over the Wye which the hotel used so prominently in its brochure. Probably, he thought, the latter, for the panorama they came upon so suddenly at the corner of the old building was both spectacular and uplifting.

They were probably two hundred feet above the river, which wound its way in a leisurely horseshoe through the rich green base of the valley, as it had done for thousands of years. It was a stretch which might have been designed to illustrate the fascination of water in a view. At the extremes to right and left, where the river curved in wide reaches until it disappeared beneath trees, its deep blue was so undisturbed that it might almost have been static. But at its nearest point, where it squeezed the golf course to its narrowest width below the professional's shop, the waters rushed in a gentle turbulence over an ancient and long-disused ford, so that the water whitened and sparkled in the bright sun. It was near enough and their surroundings were quiet enough for them to catch that most ancient and beguiling sound known to the ears of men: the sound of water swirling and chuckling over stones.

Beyond the quadrangles of residences was a bowling green where a sprinkler made miniature rainbows against the sun. Here three men sat on a bench with their backs to the buildings, looking over the edge of the green to the beauty of the river and its valley. Lambert recognized the natural tonsure of George Goodman easily, then from closer quarters the grey-flecked ginger of Sandy Munro and the longer golden locks of Tony Nash.

One of the byproducts of a murder inquiry is to make those who are investigated feel sensitive about innocent actions which they feel will be observed and misinterpreted. Lambert, wondering now if the earnest colloquy of these three men carried sinister implications, realized that the corresponding strain in those who investigated was to suspect conspiracy where harmless and desultory conversation was probably all that existed.

Goodman's first words might have been designed to underline how ridiculous were such assumptions. He was the first to see Lambert and Hook. He called, 'Good morning, gentlemen!' and came forward to receive them like a genial host. 'This is a pleasant place to be incarcerated, is it not?' He gestured with a wide arm at the natural glories behind him. 'I can understand that you should wish us to see out the time we had booked here, and of course we are only too anxious to see this matter cleared up.'

Lambert had remained noncommittal for as long as possible: it was always interesting to ascertain whether suspects would reveal things about their state of mind by talking too much, even when their matter was trivial. He said with a smile, 'We find that respectable citizens like you are always anxious to help.'

'Do you think it was murder?' Tony Nash spat the question like one weary of insincere exchanges. After Goodman's half-humorous circumlocutions, his directness seemed the more stark. His right hand grasped his left forearm unnaturally hard, as if it was the only way he could keep his limbs still. The stance made Lambert alter his plans for his first interview of the day.

'I'm afraid certain things about this death point that way. You wouldn't expect me to go into detail. You'll hear what they are clearly enough at the inquest, I expect. As one of the discoverers of the corpse, you'll be asked to give evidence, of course.'

There was no need yet to tell them that Harrington had crashed to his death on the gravel; there was always the chance that guilty men might betray themselves by revealing knowledge they should not have. But he thought wryly that all his suspects were intelligent enough to make the obvious deductions from the elaborately cordoned areas around the house.

Nash looked very tense at the thought of the inquest. It was Goodman who said, like a tactful man changing a delicate subject, 'We've just decided that as we have to be here, we might as well play golf, as we intended to do before this tragedy. Unfortunately, we now find ourselves one short of the four-ball we expected to play. We can play three, of course, but I'm afraid we should always be conscious then of our missing colleague. I don't suppose you would have the time or the inclination to join us for a game some time, Superintendent? Your Inspector told us you were a single figure man.'

Goodman managed the deprecating smile very well. As a JP, it said, he was thoroughly at

111

home with policemen and police procedure. He would demonstrate to those less acquainted with these things that the innocent had nothing to fear. What gave him away were the startled glances which his two companions could not control. This was his initiative alone, not a joint one.

Lambert was for a moment as disconcerted as they were. At once amused and aghast, he found himself picturing the faces of Bert Hook and Christopher Rushton if he played. Not to mention that of the Chief Constable if he came to hear of it, as he undoubtedly would. It was unthinkable that he should accept the invitation.

'I should be delighted,' he said. 'If the circumstances of the investigation permit it.' He noted with satisfaction the dismay of Nash and Munro, even perhaps a fleeting surprise on the urbane features of Goodman that his bluff should be called so promptly. He did not dare to glance at Hook. 'Not this morning, though. Perhaps I might join you for a game this afternoon, if my schedule will allow it?'

'That would be admirable, Superintendent.' If Goodman's equilibrium had indeed been shaken, there was no sign of it when he spoke. 'We'll play a few holes on our own this morning, then hope to see you on the tee at, shall we say, two-fifteen?'

'I shall look forward to that,' said Lambert, drawn into the conventional courtesies even in these bizarre circumstances. 'But I'm afraid I must deprive you of Mr Nash for a while: I need to check his recollection of events on the night of the death.'

Nash must have known this would come sooner or later, but he looked thoroughly miserable about it, like a man answering the summons he has long expected to the dentist's chair. It was left to Goodman to answer suavely, 'Of course, of course. We shall look forward to your company this afternoon, Mr Lambert, if duties permit.'

'I should be ready for you in about a quarter of an hour, Mr Nash,' said Lambert. He turned swiftly on his heel and left them; Bert Hook followed him with what he hoped was a deadpan face. This ridiculous game clearly upset the judgement of people who should know much better by now. Ahead of him, Lambert was nursing the thought that it would be interesting to study the interactions of those three in a supposedly relaxed context; he wondered how far that was a rationalization of his impulsive acceptance of Goodman's invitation.

He was well on his way to the Murder Room before he noticed Sergeant Johnson, who was in charge of the Scene of Crime team. The officer had that indefinable air of importance which stiffens the back of men charged with news. He was standing by the corner of a long, single-storey brick building which must once

113

have been stables but now accommodated a variety of golf-course machinery and other implements. Lambert went over to examine the object which was the source of his restrained excitement.

It was a heavy wooden wheelbarrow, with a steel rim on its single heavy wheel. Probably fifty years old and dating from the days of the private estate, its sturdy workmanship proclaimed that it was good for many years of service yet. But it had now fulfilled its single dramatic function in this long working life.

For Johnson said, 'This is the means employed to move the body, sir.' He was already anticipating the convoluted phrasing of the courtroom. 'The wheel fits the only tracks found within twenty yards of the body. And forensic have just confirmed that the fibres we found at each end of this came from the back of Harrington's cardigan and trousers.'

Both of them gazed for a moment at the unremarkable contrivance that had suddenly been invested with a sickly glamour. It was all too easy to picture Harrington's heavy torso bouncing over the hard ground at dead of night in its last cradle, his legs dangling grotesquely between the handles smooth with use, his eyes gazing unseeingly at the cold stars above.

But they were policemen both. Their thoughts sprang quickly to speculation about the last hands to have gripped those shining, innocent handles.

CHAPTER TWELVE

Tony Nash was not at ease.

When he came into the interview room, it was his attempt to seem relaxed which drew attention to his discomfort. He sat down quickly in the chair indicated to him and folded his arms; his fingers moved nervously over his sweater sleeves. Hook watched them playing their repetitive tune against the light blue lambswool, wondering whether their owner could still control them if he chose.

Nash had the wide shoulders of a powerful, stocky man. Lambert, looking at the longish blond hair with its hint of disarray, was reminded of a cinema Tarzan he thought he had long forgotten. Nash was handsome enough to carry such a part: his features had the regular lines of a romantic novel's cover. Except that there was something just slightly wrong about this fresh-faced beauty: the features were infinitesimally too small for the head and the shoulders beneath them. The prettiness of a woman's face sat where something more rugged and durable might have been expected.

The end of a pink tongue moistened the

delicate lips and Nash said, 'I am only too anxious to help, of course, Superintendent, but I very much doubt if I can add much to what you already know.'

It was a conventional opening, but delivered flatly enough to reveal it as a prepared sentiment. Perhaps he expected Lambert to say, 'Best let us be the judges of that, Mr Nash.' If so, he was disappointed, for the Superintendent did no more than nod an acknowledgement, as if he had scarcely registered the thought. Then he said, 'I take it that you came here this week for no other purpose than to play golf, Mr Nash?'

Nash was immediately disconcerted. Probably it was merely by the directness of Lambert's approach, but he might have suspected a reference to his nocturnal activities with the striking Miss Peters. He said, 'That was the primary purpose for all the men. Meg doesn't play. Alison Munro does, but she hasn't been playing this week.'

'Quite. I understand that you are sharing a double room with Miss Peters.'

'Yes, but that is surely hardly—'

'I ask only because we must be sure of the disposition of the party at the time of Mr Harrington's death, Mr Nash. You must be aware that that is a point of crucial importance.'

Nash relaxed, it seemed by a deliberate effort of will. 'Yes, I see. You mean that we might be able to clear each other of any involvement in this business.'

'Possibly. Unless of course you planned the business together.' Lambert, though he knew it ignoble, enjoyed the suggestion and the concern it caused his hearer.

'I didn't kill Guy. And neither did Meg.' Nash's fingers had at last stopped moving; they were gripping tight on his upper arms, so that he looked like a child made to fold his arms against his will.

'Perhaps not. You will appreciate that we shall probably only be certain about that when we arrest the person who did. If you are not involved, your best policy will be to conceal absolutely nothing. I'm already collecting lies like blackberries in this investigation.' He did not care whether or not it was an exaggeration. He had no intention of indulging in preliminary fencing with this man.

Nash looked agreeably startled. His blue eyes widened a little and he said as aggressively as he could, 'I see. Well, you certainly haven't collected any from me.' Then he grinned weakly as the realization struck him and said, 'But then, we've hardly spoken yet.'

'Scarcely at all. Tell me, Mr Nash, did you see anything in your first two days here that seems significant now, in the light of Mr Harrington's violent death?'

'No. Nothing at all.' He seemed immediately aware that he had spoken too quickly to have given the matter proper thought, for his faced flushed in the silence the two experienced men opposite him allowed him to hang on his abrupt denial. But he had the sense not to fill the silence with any imprudent disclosure. He was intelligent, with the shrewdness that came from twenty years of successful work at a variety of levels: he was not going to be ruffled as easily as his initial demeanour had indicated.

Lambert reminded himself wearily that the innocent as well as the guilty were made nervous by police inquiries. He said, 'And yet you must have been with Guy Harrington for most of the time.'

'I suppose so. We played golf most of the day, and ate together in the evenings.'

'In all probability you conducted one or both of these activities with the person who killed your friend. So you can see the importance of my question.'

'It needn't have been one of us.'

'Indeed not. There are other possibilities, and they are being investigated. That is why I said "in all probability".'

'And he wasn't my friend.' This was an unexpected assertion; even if they had suspected it, it was unusual for someone close to a murdered man to confess so much so boldly. 'I worked for him, that was all. He was all right to play golf with, most of the time.'

'Was he a good employer?' This was Bert

118

Hook, coming in when their subject had almost forgotten him, and as usual disconcerting him by the unexpectedness of the intervention. Bert, who had moved straight from his Barnardo's home into the world of men at the age of sixteen, knew a good deal about the habits of employers, good and bad.

'No. The best thing was to keep well out of his way and get on with your job.' Hook reflected that many men had made themselves rich by encouraging that philosophy among the men they payed. 'He was a bastard. Took all he could get from you, then let you down.'

'How?' said Lambert sharply.

Nash looked like a man who had gone further than he meant to, but realized that he could scarcely draw back now. 'I'm his Sales Manager in the plastics division. I worked it up from nothing. The products were good enough, but they needed selling, like anything else. When I'd done all the hard work, he pegged my salary. That didn't worry me that much—I thought it was time to move on anyway. But when I tried, I got nowhere. Not even interviews. Eventually I found he was writing references which ensured no one would even look at me.'

'Did you tackle him about it?'

Nash gave a mirthless laugh and a brief, hopeless gesture at the ceiling with his hands; it was the first time he had unclasped his arms since he had struck the pose when he sat down. 'I did. All he was interested in was how I'd got the information. Fortunately, it was from a secretary who had already left, so there was no way he could get at her. He said my job with him was safe for life—just so long as sales targets were achieved and I didn't step out of line. But I could forget about moving elsewhere: he didn't train up staff in order to pass them on when they were becoming useful.'

Lambert reflected that it was scarcely the kind of man-management calculated to increase profits in the long term. But such attitudes were not so unusual in small firms, even in the 'nineties. And of course, he was hearing only one side of the story. The dead were never able to defend their actions. Even taken at face value, this grievance seemed scarcely the kind to drive a man to murder.

As if reading his thoughts, the man opposite him said, 'I didn't kill him for that. I didn't even stop playing golf with him, as you can see.' He ran a hand impulsively through his mane of hair, a gesture of release from the physical tension that had built steadily in him as he talked of his dead employer. His face was full of bitterness, part of it seemingly against himself for his sycophancy.

'Were you the only one who felt like this about him?'

Nash had the confidence for the first time to pause and weigh his reply. 'No. Sandy Munro

120

doesn't say much, but I think he felt as resentful as I did about Harrington as an employer. I couldn't tell you exactly why.' Lambert, who had been told some of the reasons by Munro himself on the previous evening, merely nodded.

Nash, apparently welcoming the chance to transfer the discussion from himself to others, said, 'I'm quite sure Alison Munro didn't like him, perhaps just because of the way he treated Sandy. George Goodman seemed easy enough with Harrington, but I don't know him all that well. He didn't seem particularly upset when we found the body yesterday morning, but it's not easy to tell with George.'

Lambert himself had wondered what lay behind Goodman's carefully presented serenity. It was interesting to find that men who had known him much longer still found him difficult to estimate. But the most significant point about Nash's assessment of his party was the omission. 'You must be aware that you have left out one person,' Lambert said, playing his fish gently now.

Nash's fresh face hardened with caution. 'Meg Peters had nothing to do with this.' His mouth set obstinately, like that of a child who hopes that if he repeats something often enough it will become fact.

'That is something we shall have to establish to our own satisfaction, I'm afraid,' said Lambert. He sounded friendly, almost regretful, and indeed he had sympathy enough for one he suspected was experiencing the illogicalities of extreme sexual passion: Nash was watching him with an anxiety he could not conceal. Routine police inquiries were already turning up interesting facts about Miss Peters: he wondered how much Tony Nash knew about her past. As much, he fancied, as she had chosen to tell him, but he had no idea how much that was. 'Can you tell us something about Miss Peters's previous relationship with Harrington?'

People of Tony Nash's colouring are at a disadvantage when they wish to conceal their emotions, for the movement of blood beneath the surface of pale skin is more apparent than in others. That blood drained away now, leaving Tony Nash's cheeks suddenly sallow, as he said, 'She knew him socially for several years.' Even to himself, it sounded feeble, but he did not trust himself to say more.

'Was she ever employed by him?'

'I believe she was, briefly, some years ago.'

'Do you know in what circumstances that employment was terminated?'

'No.' Nash clearly resented the question, but again could not rely on his voice. Had the room not been quiet, his monosyllable would have been inaudible.

'You are not aware of any closer relationship between the deceased and Miss Peters?'

'No!' This time Nash shouted the word, almost before the question was out. In the quiet room, it became almost a scream. In his English embarrassment, Bert Hook watched the drip on the tap in the corner of the room grow large, detach itself, and fall soundlessly into the small basin. Lambert reflected on the perversity of human passions. This man had come into the room as a shallow figure, brittle beneath his surface beauty. Now, with that shell easily broken, he was paradoxically raised by his passion to something more distinctly human: he was suddenly Othello on the rack, contemplating in public something he had shied away from previously even in private. When Nash realized that neither of his tormentors was going to speak, he said hopelessly, 'You'll have to ask her about all that yourself.'

'Indeed, I'm afraid we shall,' said Lambert. 'Murder inquiries simply do not allow secrets, you see. Though of course many of them prove irrelevant in the end. Now, please tell us about your own relationship with Miss Peters.'

Perhaps Nash was surprised by Lambert's briskly matter-of-fact tone; perhaps he was merely relieved to pass on from the painful area of Harrington's dealings with Meg Peters. He said unhesitatingly, 'We're lovers.'

It was a word dropped too lightly as the end of the century approached, thought Lambert. It covered anything from long-term partnerships to breathy couplings in the backs of cars that were no more than the sating of an instinct. The CID needed something more precise. As if in response to his thoughts, Tony Nash looked at the carpet between them and said, 'Serious lovers. We shall be getting married in due course.'

Lambert wondered what that 'in due course' disguised. How many other lives would be lacerated to achieve this marriage? That was not and could not be his concern. He said, 'So Miss Peters feels as seriously about this as you do?'

'Ask her!' For a moment, Nash was an adolescent, confident and proud in the strength of his first grand passion. It was enviable in a man in his forties, however dangerous it might be. But it lasted only a moment: then he felt the need to explain himself in an older man's terms. 'Neither of us expected it to get serious. But it is, and it will last.'

Lambert had heard such protestations too often to react positively. He looked at Nash like a postman estimating an unreliable dog: he wanted to get at the truth of his next query without provoking an outburst of passionate protestation. He said, 'Let's move closer to the time of Harrington's death. I understand that there was a dispute between you and him during your final meal together.'

'I knew you'd have to rake this over.' Nash

muttered the complaint to himself rather than to his questioner; he had known they must come to this. Indeed, Sandy Munro had told him only an hour before that he had had to speak of it to the Superintendent.

'I shall rake this and any other conflict over as thoroughly as I can. Don't forget the man you clashed with was dead within three or four hours. I'll need to be convinced that this incident had nothing to do with his death. By you or by someone else.'

Nash nodded, tight-lipped. 'It had nothing to do with his death. He said something about Meg and I took exception to it, that's all.'

'What kind of thing?'

'He called her a tart.'

'In so many words?'

'Oh no, he was far too clever for that!' Nash's bitterness started out again as he reviewed the incident and the picture it presented of him as a naïve hot-head. 'He tried to pass it off as a joke, but I wasn't having that. I made him apologize.' He was a strange mixture of embarrassed recollection and pride in what he had done.

Lambert decided not to press him further on the detail of the incident; there were others who could give him that. Not least of them Meg Peters herself. He filed away the thought that the man before him would certainly have been capable of the sudden, violent action that had produced the death of Guy Harrington. 'I should like you to recall the end of that evening for us now.'

He had judged it right. Nash moved almost eagerly from the confrontation at the dinner-table to events in the last hour or two of Harrington's life. 'We sat out on the flat roof drinking a bottle of brandy. It was warm enough to do that, even towards midnight.'

'And no doubt the brandy helped to keep the chill at bay.'

'We were none of us drunk.'

Lambert smiled grimly. 'I'm glad to hear there is no chance of a plea of diminished responsibility on that score. But the bottle must have circulated fairly freely: there wasn't much of it left when we examined it yesterday. And quite a lot of wine had been consumed with the meal.'

Nash considered the matter carefully, as if the idea that someone might have been drunk, might have killed Harrington accidentally, was an attractive possibility that he had not previously entertained. 'We'd eaten a heavy meal. I don't think anyone had had a real skinful. We were happy rather than drunk.'

'You didn't see anyone becoming aggressive?'

'Rather the reverse. Most people became quite mellow.'

Or appeared so to you, thought Bert Hook. His resistance to the bourgeoisie was surfacing despite his attempts at objectivity. These privileged people, playing this decadent game of golf all week and indulging in *la dolce vita* off the course, had fostered a rottenness at the heart of their gathering. He looked up from his notebook and said, 'What happened to you when the group finally broke up, Mr Nash?'

Nash thought carefully; once they had moved off the area of his emotional involvement, he was almost the ideal court witness, weighing his thoughts carefully before he spoke, trying to keep to the subject of the question but give the fullest possible reply. Or else, of course, he was presenting that persona very carefully, as a murderer might do. 'It was George Goodman, I think, who made the first move; he said it was long past his normal bedtime and he would suffer on the course in the morning if he didn't make a move. Sandy Munro went off almost at the same time—I thought to his room, but he tells me this morning he went for a walk down the drive. The two ladies went off together: I thought at the time to the cloakroom, but of course they may not have done.' He paused.

'And you?'

'I stayed on the roof with Harrington for a few minutes.'

'Why was that?'

'I'm not sure. Perhaps it was no more than lethargy at the end of a long day. I think I had some idea that Guy might want to smooth things over after our spat earlier in the

127

evening.'

'And did he?'

'No. Perhaps I was a bit drunk after all, to think he would. We never exchanged a word. We sat looking over the edge of the roof for a few minutes. I remember seeing the bend of the river by the sixteenth fairway quite clearly. Guy didn't say anything, but he gave me a superior sort of grin, as if he was challenging me to take up where we left off. I just got up and left, without even saying good night.'

A very sensible course of action. If it happened. Lambert said quietly, 'You were therefore the last person to see Harrington alive.'

'Apart from his murderer.' Nash managed a small, apologetic grin. Lambert liked him the better for it.

'As you say. Did you see anyone else after you left the roof?'

'No.'

'Did you go straight back to your room?'

'Not quite. I went out to the car park. I wanted to check that I'd put my clubs away properly in the back of the car.'

'And had you?' If the man was fabricating a story, he was most likely to trip up over detail he might not have rehearsed.

'Almost. I had put the clubs away all right, but forgotten to lock the boot of the car.'

'Make and model?' said Hook, ballpoint poised.

'Ford Granada. This year's model.' He looked puzzled by the question.

Lambert knew the point well enough. But there was no discrepancy: the boot did indeed need locking, though it could be done by means of the car's central locking system. Some cheaper and older cars had boots which locked automatically when the lid was put down. He said, 'What would you estimate was the total time between the others leaving you with Harrington and your returning to your room?'

'I couldn't be sure. At the time, I obviously didn't think it was important. Perhaps a quarter of an hour.'

'Did you see anyone while you were in the car park?'

'No. I expect Sandy Munro was well away, down towards the gate somewhere.'

'And when you got back to your room, was Miss Peters already there?'

Nash hesitated. 'I met her at the door.'

'Do you know where she had been?'

'No. I presumed at the time she had been with Alison Munro. But I didn't ask. There was no reason why it should have been important, at the time.'

'No. I have to ask you formally now, Mr Nash, whether you have any thoughts about who might have brought about this death. Needless to say, we will respect your confidence.'

'No.' Nash looked thoroughly disturbed; perhaps he had not really contemplated head on the notion of murder by one of their group until that moment. Then, in a burst of confidence, he said, 'I'm not at all sure that I'd tell you if I did.'

Lambert gave him a sour smile. 'That would be most unwise, Mr Nash. It would make you an accessory after the fact of murder. I must remind you that it is your duty to come to us immediately if anything occurs to you which might seem to have a bearing on this most serious of crimes.'

Nash levered himself easily from the chair by the use of his powerful forearms, but he looked as chastened as a schoolboy as he was dismissed. Lambert was still gathering his thoughts and watching Hook complete his record of the interview in his round, careful hand when there was the most discreet of taps at the door.

Sergeant Johnson, head of the Scene of Crime team, came almost apologetically into the room. 'It's Inspector Rushton's day off. We've just had a message through from Forensic. I thought you'd like the news right away, as soon as you'd finished your interview.' Johnson had got Lambert attacked and almost killed by his failure to pass on a vital message in the previous year [*Bring Forth Your Dead*]: he still addressed him as if in perpetual expectation of a reprimand.

'Well?' Lambert was disgusted with himself that he should be so pleased that it was not Rushton who had collected this news.

'They've analysed the strips taken from the corpse's clothing, along with other samples. There are fibres which indicate someone else has handled the body. Presumably the person who lifted it on to the wheelbarrow and moved it. The position of the fibres, on the lower back, indicates that someone—'

'Who?'

'The fibres appear to be from the sweater worn on that evening by Sandy Munro.'

CHAPTER THIRTEEN

Detective-Inspector Christopher Rushton was one of the modern breed of husbands. He shared the household chores, changed nappies, and on his day off he sometimes even helped his wife with the shopping.

He was also a policeman, and policemen are notoriously conservative animals. Rushton was sufficiently affected by his calling to be diffident about declaring his enlightenment in domestic matters. It was all very well to be acclaimed a pillar of the campaign against chauvinism among his wife's friends, but the same qualities could declare him a wimp at Oldford CID headquarters, where the male ethos was still overwhelmingly predominant.

Consequently, Rushton cast the occasional furtive glance over his shoulder as he pushed the slowly filling supermarket trolley between the avenues of tins and packets. None of his colleagues was apparent; even the store detectives did not recognize him these days, now that his exalted rank had lifted him so far above the petty, amateur crime of shoplifting.

He watched the features of the checkout girl, scarcely more expressive than the electronic read-out on her till, then admired his wife's small, expert hands, as they stowed the produce in her bags so much more quickly than his own larger and stronger ones. He pushed the trolley to the boot of the Sierra, unloaded the bags into the car, assessed the number of his Brownie points, and wondered what to do with the rest of his day off.

It was an unpleasant shock when his wife said, 'What are you going to do with yourself for the next hour?' He must have looked blank, for she said, 'You haven't forgotten my appointment at the Health Centre, have you?'

Of course he had, though he remembered swiftly enough now. She was engaging in preventive medicine at the 'Well Woman Clinic'. Her mother was staying with them, looking after Kirstie for the morning; her presence in the house partly explained his presence here, though he had argued more worthy and altruistic motives. He said with a grin, 'Would I forget, Anne?' Then, on impulse and before she could offer an opinion, 'I thought I might have a look round the Cathedral for a while.'

If she was surprised, she gave no sign of it. He walked through some of the older streets of Hereford until the Cathedral rose unexpectedly before him, like a great ship in dock. Matins was long over, and the cool quiet of the place enveloped him; the nave was like a vast, civilized cave. He raised his eyes to the great tower that he knew was one of the features of the building and tried to recall what he had read of this place in the book he had at home. He remembered that the west front had collapsed a couple of centuries ago and that the restoration was not approved by modern pundits: little else would come back to him at first.

If Bert Hook was doing an Open University degree, the DI who directed him had better look to his academic laurels: he resolved at least to bring himself up to date on his local cathedral. It was no hardship: this was a pleasant enough place to be on a May morning. He sat on a bench, felt the serenity of nine centuries in the silent stones which soared above him, and was glad he had come here. He fell to calculating whether he had yet become an agnostic, decided he was still C. of E. with severe reservations, and wondered how much ground lay between these two theological positions.

There were not many people about to disturb his spiritual deliberations. The tourist season was not yet at its height, and the first great publicity impact of the 1989 controversy over the proposed sale of the cathedral's *Mappa Mundi* was over. He looked at the vaulted roof, so impossibly high above him; a line about singing masons building roofs of gold came back to him he knew not whence.

He was gratified: this place was conducive to the recovery of such long-forgotten, disregarded things. There was after all much more to life than being a policeman, even a successful one. He sat very still. And eventually from the recesses of Christopher Rushton's mind there crept the remembrance that the Lady Chapel was one of the oldest parts of this ancient building.

He was ludicrously pleased by the rediscovery of this simple and unremarkable fact. His brain cells were still present in plenty and doing their job. He looked automatically towards the entrance to the Lady Chapel.

And became in an instant a policeman again.

There was a woman there whom he had seen before. A tall woman; fiftyish; about a hundred and thirty pounds; with plentiful, well coiffured grey hair. Despite her height, her navy leather shoes had quite high heels; her dark blue dress was soberly but expensively cut, its elegance complemented by the small handbag she carried on her left forearm.

He thought he had seen her only once before: probably in a professional rather than a social context. His mind ran through the cases he was currently concerned with. There were no more than three: this was the advantage of being 'concerned only with serious crime'. That was the way his wife's mother always introduced him, explaining away the presence of a policeman in the family. He smiled wryly, hearing her apologetic tones in his head.

In the same instant, he knew the woman. He had glimpsed her only briefly and never spoken to her. But he felt he should instantly have placed her: for years, he had driven himself to promotion by being unforgiving with himself, until it had now become a habit. He had seen her with that supercilious sod Lambert, walking round the golf course at the Wye Castle. It was typical of the Super, who sometimes seemed to break the rules just for the sake of doing so, that he should have allowed her to identify the body on site.

For this woman was, or had been, Mrs Guy Harrington. Marie Harrington, he had better say, if his image as enlightened man was to be preserved. He remembered making a mental note to emphasize the second syllable of that 'Marie'. The sober colours of her dress might pass for mourning, he supposed: he was no expert in these things. But she carried no badge of bereavement, and her bearing was not that of a heartbroken widow. She moved a few paces across the front of the Lady Chapel, then back again to her first position, staring at the stained glass with unseeing eyes.

She was looking at her watch when the man arrived to meet her. They exchanged brief, tight smiles and moved away into the deserted Lady Chapel. As Rushton moved softly over cool stone to observe them, they sat together in a pew towards the front of this ancient place of devotion. They had not touched each other throughout these movements.

If it had taken the Inspector's trained mind a moment to place the woman, his recognition of the man who had come here to meet her was instantaneous. As indeed it should have been, for he had taken a first, brief statement from him as the discoverer of a body scarcely more than twenty-four hours earlier.

George Goodman seemed to fit naturally into this place, in his clerical grey suit and shining black shoes. His white hair encircled his tanned bald head in a way that seemed reassuringly traditional, even when viewed from the rear. Thus might a Victorian burgher have sat a hundred years earlier. Thus, with suit exchanged for a habit, might a medieval monk have meditated and prayed when peasants peered in at this place and marvelled at a new architectural wonder of the world.

Except that Goodman was not praying. Of that Rushton was sure, though he could detect no syllable of what passed between the pair. Their exchanges were sporadic, terse and urgent, between prolonged silences. For a long time, Marie Harrington did not look at the man beside her. Then she turned quite suddenly to look at him, staring hard at his face from a distance of no more than two feet. After a moment, she placed a small white hand gently on top of the back of his larger one.

Goodman did not respond: he remained staring fixedly at the altar ahead. Through the tawdry nineteenth-century stained glass which had been mistakenly added to the chapel, a shaft of sunlight threw a sudden iridescence upon the pair. For a moment they were frozen like a detail from an old master on a religious theme. Then the clouds returned, and their moment of transient, unconscious glory passed like a vision in a storm.

The only witness of it glided softly behind one of the vast pillars of the nave as the little tableau began to disintegrate. George Goodman and Marie Harrington moved swiftly out through the north door. Their watcher followed, discreetly distant, through the narrow streets around the Cathedral and into the more modern and populous part of the town. In the car park, they were swallowed into Goodman's dark blue Rover. Then the vehicle moved swiftly and almost silently from his sight and out of the town.

Detective-Inspector Rushton, on his day off, had had his attention pulled back to the investigation he had left behind him. Policemen, as he was fond of reminding his junior staff, are never off duty. He told himself that the rendezvous he had seen might have nothing to do with the death at the Wye Castle.

But he did not really believe himself.

CHAPTER FOURTEEN

While Rushton was watching the meeting in Hereford Cathedral, his chief was pursuing the investigation more officially three miles outside the city at the Wye Castle.

Meg Peters had a considerable presence. Bert Hook, pen poised over a pristine page of his notebook, reckoned himself something of an expert in these things, and was prepared to concede that to her immediately. She came into the room without that instant of diffidence which was natural for most people in this situation. When the two CID men rose politely, it was for a moment as if they were the subordinates, awaiting an audience which had been graciously granted to them.

She was poised and unhurried, yet businesslike. She looked round the room and

138

took the only chair which was obvious for her without its being indicated, as though she had made a choice among alternatives. She tossed her brilliant red hair as she sank gracefully down, and her musky perfume seemed to sweep in waves across the room to challenge their masculinity. Hook thought he had never known an innocent monsyllable invested with so much challenge as her opening 'Well?'

Lambert was unhurried, knowing that in any contest of wills he had all the key cards in his hand. He shuffled the papers in front of him on the desk, reflecting that he had beneath his fingers the power to humiliate this woman, if it should prove necessary. He said, 'You are human enough to have talked to the others, I'm sure, Miss Peters. So you will have a good idea what we are about and how we proceed.'

'I didn't kill Guy Harrington.' She crossed her legs as though the gesture were the formal opening move in some physical contest. Black nylon knees glinted appealingly.

'That's good.'

'And I don't know who did.'

'Indeed. Well, I suppose you may have saved us quite a lot of time by driving straight at questions we might have approached less directly.'

Her demeanour implied that she thought that she had done just that. Her green eyes were wary: she had come into the room expecting to use anger as a weapon, but found no obvious target for it yet.

'Well what's the point of all this if you believe what I say?'

Lambert pursed his lips, a mannerism he did not often indulge in, then leaned back in his chair, letting the silence stretch as he affected to collect his thoughts. He was aware of how irritated she was by the pause, as he would have been himself in the same circumstances. He had every intention of getting her rattled, having decided in advance that she was far more likely to be useful and revelatory in such a state.

When he spoke, his tone was deliberately off-hand. 'For one thing, I haven't said that I do believe what you say yet. A moment's thought will tell you that we can't simply go around accepting every simple statement of innocence people make to us. Otherwise, the proportion of serious criminals we bring to justice would be much smaller and our salaries rightly much reduced.'

His smile was bland, friendly, almost apologetic. She thought him quite insufferable; her brows contracted and the two lines between them became furrows of resentment. The fingers of her right hand twisted for a moment through the slim gold bracelet on her wrist. 'Don't play games with me, Superintendent, please. Why should you disbelieve me, more than anyone else?'

'Oh, I haven't said I do, Miss Peters. But

since you ask, there is a reason why most criminal investigators would treat your statements with more suspicion than those of the other people I have so far seen.'

'And what is that reason?' She scarcely cared to conceal her anger now. Most men consider a quick temper an attraction in redheads, perhaps as an indication of other passions swift to kindle. The human brain being the perplexing instrument that it is, Lambert found himself wondering disconcertingly how fired he might be by this woman in those other contexts. Fortunately she could not see his thoughts and reduce his eroticism to ashes with her swift contempt.

He picked up a sheet of paper and affected to study the details he already knew by heart. Then he looked steadily across his desk at the woman whose green eyes smouldered with scarcely contained hostility. 'Perhaps you are not aware that whenever we are investigating a serious crime we check the previous criminal history of those close to it. To put it bluntly, we see if any of those concerned have what you will have heard policemen call "form", Miss Peters.'

He looked at her interrogatively to see if she wished to comment; he was carefully, offensively polite as he prepared the stiletto. She was pallid now beneath the Titian waves, for she must have known what was coming. As carefully as a man pronouncing a legal formula, Lambert said, 'I have to tell you that you are the only one of your group who has a previous criminal conviction.'

Hook had needed to record nothing yet. Watching from his position two yards away from his chief, he thought Lambert sounded like the old recording of Prime Minister Chamberlain breaking the news of war in 1939. Meg Peters looked as shocked as the listeners who had needed to digest that momentous news. She licked lips that seemed suddenly garish against her pallor. 'It doesn't mean anything, in relation to Harrington.' She managed to invest the three syllables of the name with venomous contempt.

Lambert said, 'It may not do. I'm speaking generally rather than specifically, of course, but any statistician would tell you there is quite a high correlation between previous convictions and later, more serious offences. Criminal records are one of the best starting-points we have in many investigations.'

'Even when the crime is quite different and much more serious?'

'Even when the crime is murder, Miss Peters.' She gasped at the word, realizing he had enunciated the very noun she had been reluctant to acknowledge herself. Without her recognizing quite how it had happened, their positions were now reversed: Lambert was direct and aggressive after his earlier circumlocutions, and she seemed evasive by

142

comparison.

As if to emphasize her position, he said coolly, 'As a matter of fact, there is a fairly high correlation between convictions for drug offences and subsequent serious crime.'

It was the first mention of the nature of her offence. She glanced for the first time at Hook, wondering how much this silent recorder had known. He might previously have been a statue, for all the attention she had given him, and he took care now to present his best sculptured impassivity. She looked suddenly tired as she said sullenly, 'It was only for cannabis. And it was a long time ago.'

'And you weren't selling it to others. As far as anyone could prove.' There might have been a hint of irony in Lambert's even tones, but it was impossible to be certain.

She flashed him a basilisk glance of pure hate, then cast her eyes sharply down, as if she realized belatedly that they divulged too much. They were very beautiful eyes and she had used them countless times to manipulate men; it was disconcerting now to find them revealing so much she would have wished to conceal. She said, 'I never traded. I was in the theatre, and everyone used pot then.'

He knew enough for that to ring true. But there was no reason why he should concede it to her now: his task was to unmask a murderer. Or murderess; but probably that was an outdated term in these days of equality.

No doubt Ms Peters would call herself an actor. 'Perhaps your companions did use pot. But it was a criminal offence, and you were found guilty.'

'I was only twenty-one. I haven't been in court since.'

Her phrasing suggested to an ear tuned to such protestations that she had been near to it on some occasions. But perhaps she was just unfortunate in her choice of words. The conviction was fourteen years behind her: that made her thirty-five. She looked it, but she was a woman whom the years enhanced rather than reduced, up to a certain point. Her figure had not thickened at the waist, her hair was still as dazzling as in her youth, her face not yet seriously lined. It was the kind of face that experience made more exciting as it built upon the blanker beauty of youth. Lambert said, 'Did Harrington know about your drugs conviction?'

The abrupt transfer from her own problems to the central issue of the interview stilled the last of her truculence. Her troubled face revealed too much: they saw her consider whether to lie, decide against it, and say reluctantly, 'Yes.'

'How?'

She shrugged the shapely shoulders automatically. 'He knew most things.'

'And how did he come to know this one?'

'I don't know.' Now she was lying; her face

set like a child's, obstinate in denial yet not expecting to be believed.

'Was it not from your own lips?'

The green eyes, dark now with anger and apprehension, flashed to his for a moment, speculating on how much he knew. 'It might have been. But I think he knew before—'

Her voice dropped away hopelessly. It was almost a mercy when he said gently, 'Before what, Miss Peters?'

'I had an affair with Guy Harrington. I suppose you know that: you seem to know everything.' She said it bitterly, and he made no attempt to deny it. An impression that the CID were omniscient was a most useful delusion to foster in the public.

'How long ago was this?'

'It ended four years ago last month.'

Very precise: he wondered what should be deduced from that. 'And it had lasted for how long?'

'Seven months.'

Again the detail. He decided she must have expected this to come out and thought about her answers. It made him wonder how important the affair was in the case. 'Did Mrs Harrington know about this relationship?'

He had expected her to bridle before now at his impertinence; she showed no sign of doing so. 'I expect she did. She's not stupid, and I wasn't the first. Nor the last.' Her smile was at her own expense, but it lit up the pale face for a moment. That face had no doubt caused anguish to many men in its time; now it seemed to be recognizing the irony of its rejection.

That thought prompted Lambert's next question. 'Who ended the affair, Miss Peters?' She looked at him sharply at last, so that he added, 'I'm sorry to probe so far, but you will appreciate that we need to know as much as we can about the victim's past in a death of this sort.'

There was a touch of the contempt with which she had begun as she said, 'I suppose so. But you'll find this has nothing to do with it. Anyway, it was Guy who ditched me, if you must know.'

'I'm afraid I must. I appreciate your candour, Miss Peters, but I should have to ask other people about this if you refused to talk about it. It gives you, after all, a common motive for murder.'

'"*Nor hell a fury like a woman scorned,*" you mean?'

He bowed his head in unconscious acknowledgement. 'You have the quotation accurately, unlike most people who use the thought.'

'I appeared in Congreve when I was at drama school. I told you I was an actress, Mr Lambert.'

So he was wrong about that: she had chosen the term he would have used himself. He must check any other assumptions he made about her. 'About a fifth of murders in Britain involve what are loosely called "crimes of passion". So we would be wrong not to investigate any possibility of that kind. Unfortunately for the perpetrators, it is a concept treated more sympathetically in French law than in English or Scottish courts. Why did Harrington end the affair?'

He had hoped to surprise her into some revelation by the abruptness of the question, but he did not succeed. She gave a rueful smile; it was not a habitual expression for her, but it made her look very attractive. 'There was nothing very complicated about it. He moved on to pastures new. I knew I wasn't the first woman he'd had, by a long chalk. And I'd had enough experience to know better. But we all think we'll be different from the rest. Or at least that we'll be cool enough to end it in our own good time. Guy took up with a girl in his office and laughed in my face.'

'Forgive me, but detectives can't allow the dead to rest in peace. We have to build up a picture of a man who isn't here to speak for himself. I must ask you what kind of man you think Harrington was.'

Again she gave that curiously unguarded smile at herself and her foolishness. 'You don't have to apologize, Superintendent. Guy was a bastard. Attractive enough, ready with charm and money when he wanted something.

Women don't acknowledge to themselves how important money is, you know. At the time you think it's incidental, but it greases the wheels of an affair, especially in the early stages. Sometimes I'm not very fond of my own sex and the way we deceive ourselves.'

Lambert waited to see if she would enlarge upon this generality, but she merely looked at him wryly when he didn't immediately press on. Perhaps she thought she had pushed herself up the list of suspects by her bitterness about the dead man. He said, 'How much did Mrs Harrington know of her husband's activities?'

'As much as she cared to, I think. Marie is highly intelligent and pretty clear-sighted. I told you I think she knew all about our affair, though she chose not to mention it to me. Probably she knew it would run its course, like others before it.'

'How much do you think she resented her husband's activities?'

Meg Peters shrugged her beautifully rounded shoulders. 'Impossible to say. I've asked myself that before: I'm not entirely insensitive to the feelings of others. I don't know what there was left in the marriage, if anything. She doesn't give much away.'

Lambert nodded. Just as much as she cares to, he thought, remembering the elegant grey-haired woman who had been so disconcertingly insistent on identifying the body at the scene of the crime. Both she and the woman in front of him would have had the will and the drive to push a man to a mortal fall if the spirit had moved them to it. He said, 'I hope you will understand that I have to ask this. How serious is your present relationship with Mr Nash?'

For a moment he thought she was about to erupt. Then she relaxed visibly; how much this came from a conscious effort he was unable to determine. 'Very serious. We intend to get married in two months' time.'

'Will your wedding distress anyone?'

It was curiously phrased, but she understood him readily enough. 'No. Tony is already separated. I have no other serious commitments. No one will be anything but pleased, now that Harrington is dead.' She brought the idea in almost as a challenge; her small chin jutted defiantly forward beneath the full lips.

'He didn't approve of the match?'

'He approved of very little that he hadn't arranged himself. And Tony was an employee. Guy was like a mediaeval lord of the manor where they were concerned. Thought he should control everything, from their religion to whom they married. Not that he concerned himself much with religion!' she added as an afterthought.

'Why didn't he want Tony Nash to marry you?'

'I've thought about that a lot over the last few months. I think he couldn't bear that a former mistress of his, even a discarded one, should bind herself to another man. Not under his nose with one of his senior employees.'

She looked up at him anxiously, confirming his suspicion that there was more to this business than she had told him. 'And what else had he against your marriage?' he prompted gently.

The green eyes gazed steadily at her high-heeled shoes as she said, 'I don't think Guy liked the idea of his sexual preferences being leaked to one of his employees. Actually, Tony and I never speak of him, least of all in our more intimate moments, but Guy wouldn't have understood that. He was always anxious to dig the dirt on anyone himself.'

'And there were things about himself that he wouldn't have cared to reveal?'

'There are things about most of us that we wouldn't care to reveal, Mr Lambert.' For a moment it was she who was in charge and he the gauche stumbler among things he did not comprehend. She did not exploit it. 'Guy was like a lot of sexually aggressive men: secretly ashamed of what he asked in the stress of passion. He was into bondage; he was titillated by chains and leather underwear.'

It was very quiet in a room that now seemed over-warm. Bert Hook, concentrating with all his will upon his slow round handwriting, found this did not blur the vividness of the visions of the opulent Meg Peters which thrust themselves upon his mind's eye.

Lambert said, 'And you think he was afraid you would reveal his preferences to your fiancé?'

She nodded; a red tress fell over her left eye, and she brushed it impatiently away. 'I'm certain of it. And he thought Tony would have made use of the knowledge to get some kind of hold over him. He would certainly have done that himself in the same circumstances, and he couldn't believe anyone else would behave differently.'

Lambert watched her closely as he said, 'Harrington is emerging from the various conversations I've had as a decidedly unattractive character. A dangerous enemy, perhaps. Had he any means of harming you, beyond what we have already discussed?'

She looked at him in surprise; above the turquoise of her blouse, he was sure he caught fear in those wide green eyes. For a second she studied him, estimating what he might know. Then she dropped her eyes again and said softly, 'No. Nothing.'

He waited, stretching the moment, hoping the tension would draw her into something more revealing. He said with minatory severity, 'It would be far better to tell us everything now, Miss Peters. You have already been very helpful.'

'Too helpful, it seems.' She was almost back to her opening hostility. 'All my frankness has done is to make you press me for information I do not have.'

There was enough actress in her for her angry disdain to carry some conviction, but she did not meet his eyes as she had done earlier. He was convinced there was something more, but equally certain that he would not extract it now, for her lips had set in a determined line. He wondered if any of the others in the group knew what it was that she was so anxious to conceal. It must be very personal, in view of what she had already revealed.

He said abruptly, 'Tell me about the quarrel between Harrington and your fiancé during his last meal.'

Perhaps he was piqued by her refusal to tell him more, for the question was delivered like a sudden slap across the face. But she showed only relief at the return to an area she had expected to speak about. 'Tony took exception on my behalf to one of Guy's insults. He should have known better, but it was sweet of him.'

'What exactly did Harrington say?'

'I'm not sure of the precise words. I don't think I caught them, even at the time. But in effect, Guy called me a tart.'

'And you reacted angrily?'

Her smile had a touch of disdain for a man who could think her so predictable. 'On the contrary, I refused to be drawn. I had seen Guy play his games too often to react in the way he wanted. Unfortunately, Tony felt compelled to defend my honour.' Her use of the conventional phrase implied derision, but her smile was full of fondness for a headstrong lover who could react with such adolescent outrage.

'I understand he made Harrington apologize for his remarks.'

'He did indeed. I was grateful, but it was unnecessary.'

'Are you sure you can't recall exactly what those remarks were?'

She coloured a little as she said, 'I'm afraid I can't, Superintendent. Surely the exact words aren't crucial?'

He was sure she remembered them perfectly, and her reticence quickened his interest in their importance. No one else had been able to give him the exact words which had provoked Nash's outburst, or even recall the nature of the insult. If it had been personal to Meg Peters, perhaps only she had understood the sharpness of this particular shaft. And she was keeping the information to herself.

Lambert said crisply, 'You will understand on reflection that I must be interested in the last conflict of a man who was murdered four hours later. If you or Mr Nash suddenly recall the words which caused that dispute, no doubt you will convey them to us immediately. Now, would you please give me an account of your movements when the party broke up at the end of the evening?'

'Most of us had drunk quite a lot.' She was the first one to have admitted that. 'I went for a pee as soon as we broke up.' She spoiled whatever effect she intended by glancing up to see if he was shocked. For years he had operated in city slums, where such phrasing might be considered a euphemism; now he did not even acknowledge it. 'Then I went back to our room. Tony was already there.'

That was volunteered too readily: she had been determined to say it, as if it offered him a kind of alibi. And it did not tally with his account: he had said that he had met her at the door. He said, 'You're sure of that?'

'Quite sure.' It came a little too pat, with no pause for thought. Perhaps she had not been a very good actress: with the advantage of her striking looks, she should perhaps have made more of an impact than she had.

'How long was this after the party broke up for the night?' This time she did think, or affect to do so. 'Perhaps twenty minutes. I couldn't be exact.'

'Of course not. And how was the rest of the time occupied, after you had emptied your bladder?'

He was more successful in surprising her than she had been with him. She looked at him quickly, then grinned ruefully, as if accepting that she had been outsmarted in a small, irrelevant game. Then she said, resolutely unembarrassed, 'We unmarried women are a little more careful than wives when we present ourselves to our lovers at night. It was probably no more than vanity, but I spent a little time with my comb and my make-up case in the cloakroom, making myself as presentable as I could to meet Tony in our bedroom.'

It afforded her no alibi; it was also lame and touching enough for him to consider it might well be true. He nodded and said, 'Think very carefully, please. Did you see or hear anything after you had left the roof garden which might have any bearing on the death which followed?'

She hesitated. 'It's probably nothing to do with the death.'

'Quite possibly. If so, it will harm no one.'

She nodded. 'All right. The cloakroom is only one floor below the roof garden. When I came out, I heard raised voices from the roof where we had all been sitting. It sounded like an argument. To be accurate, it sounded like a hell of a row. I couldn't hear any words, and I didn't hang around to try. But I could hear the voices. One of them was Harrington's.'

She stopped, needing the prompt to lead her on to the revelation. He could not tell whether her reluctance was natural or simulated. He said, fulfilling his role, 'And whose was the other voice?'

'Alison Munro's.'

CHAPTER FIFTEEN

Superintendents are not supposed to feel guilt. A thick skin is supposed to develop around conscience and other sensibilities as they move up through the ranks.

Lambert found that he had not developed it to the appropriate pachyderm thickness. Assembling with three murder suspects for an afternoon's golf, he found himself snatching glances at the wide window of the murder room behind him, wondering what curious eyes and trenchant comments lurked behind it. A Super capable of such eccentric departures must surely invite censure, but the glass stared blankly back at him, like the eye of a monster robot observing and recording his dubious conduct.

He was not afraid that his seniors might see and reprimand him. If the Chief Constable chose to question his methods, he would be answered dismissively by a man who had decided that he had risen quite high enough in the hierarchy for his tastes. What Lambert found disconcerting was the realization that he could still be so sensitive about what his subordinates thought of his actions. He was irritatingly relieved to remember that this was the strait-laced Rushton's day off. The punctilious Inspector would never have approved of this proceeding, he was sure. And of course Lambert would never have stooped to explanations.

'You've drawn the short straw I'm afraid, John. You're playing with me!' The mellow tones of George Goodman drew him back to matters in hand and told him that for a few hours at least his first name, not his title, would be resolutely used by his companions.

'If you believe that, you're too credulous for a policeman!' said Tony Nash, retrieving the balls which had been thrown into the air to determine partners in the four-ball and handing Lambert's back to him. 'Thank God I've got Sandy with me to provide the steadiness.'

Munro grinned a tight acknowledgement of this tribute to his skills. He seemed of the three the one most aware of the incongruity of this situation, where hunter was to consort for the afternoon with the hunted, while all of them pretended that amusement was all they sought. His reserve set Lambert wondering what if anything he would learn from this bizarre three hours' traffic on the golf course. He for one would not be forsaking his calling, and he doubted that any of them expected him to do so.

He would study his three companions with interest. If one of them was a murderer, he would be intensely wary. But that in itself would be noticeable and significant, since presumably the other two would be freer and more natural in their exchanges. That was the sort of consideration that had made him accept Goodman's invitation in the first place. He told himself that as he sniffed the warm air and swung his driver at the head of a daisy with anticipatory enthusiasm.

In fact, the afternoon proceeded more freely than any of them had a right to expect. For the first two holes, their exchanges seemed edgy and artificial. Then the rhythms and challenges of the game began to blunt the edges of embarrassment, and the four of them behaved on the surface at least much as they might have done in a friendly game set in a more normal framework. Lambert was reminded of the occasions when the police video-recorded soccer crowds or city processions. For a few moments, people were intensely self-conscious. Then, surprisingly quickly, they forgot the presence of the cameras and became absorbed in their immediate concerns, even when these were sometimes highly questionable.

Golf and its handicap system demanded their concentration. Munro was easily the best player, but Goodman at his own level was almost as steady. Receiving several shots from the taciturn and skilful Scot, he was content to play within his limitations and await his opportunities. Lambert and Nash had games which kind commentators might have described as mercurial and more realistic ones as erratic. Each was likely to disappear from a hole completely, leaving his partner to salvage what he might, but each was capable of the occasional surprising success.

Lambert, who described himself as a 'rather optimistic' nine handicap, was enjoying one of his better days. The slice which was his natural shot was under control for most of the time, and he took the third hole with a long putt for an unlikely birdie. The May sun seemed suddenly even brighter, the sky an incredible, Mediterranean blue, the air alpine in its freshness. The murder room was out of sight, the investigation for a moment out of mind.

It could not last, of course. He caught Sandy Munro studying him surreptitiously while Goodman prepared to drive from the next tee, and was instantly back among the questions which remained to be answered about these three. Munro and his wife must surely have compared notes, in which case they must by now be aware of the discrepancy in their stories about the night of the murder. Munro had said that he had found Alison in bed when he had returned from his midnight walk; she had said that he was in bed and asleep when she had returned.

Munro flighted a two-iron to the edge of the next green as Lambert watched enviously. He could not know yet that he had left fibres from his sweater on the clothing of the murder victim. He was wearing that very sweater now: Lambert made a mental note that they must obtain it as police evidence before much longer. The Scot was a remarkably cool customer, guilty or innocent. No one else got anywhere near that green, into the wind; Munro rolled his long putt to within three inches of his target and took the hole with a minimum of fuss.

For a murderer, the ability to behave coolly under pressure and assess the odds with accuracy in any situation would be valuable attributes. For a moment, Lambert toyed with the attractive and romantic notion of games as deliberators of character. Then experience drove him back to reality. He had seen too many chivalrous games-players who battered their wives to place any reliance on such parallels.

Nor could he deduce anything useful from the play and bearing of the other two participants in this Kafkaesque exercise. Tony Nash seemed unguarded enough in his responses, preoccupied with the problems of his own game. By his own admission, he was the last man known to have been with Harrington, after the others had gone their separate ways at the end of that fateful evening, and he had quarrelled with him with startling if transitory violence during the meal. Yet his cheerful string of oaths when he despatched a ball into the river seemed totally unforced, a perfectly natural reaction for a violent man under stress.

Lambert noted his assumption of a natural violence in this broad-shouldered, powerful man. And how much did Nash know of the background of Meg Peters and her previous relationship with the dead man? How much, for that matter, had she held back about herself and what Harrington knew of her? He was sure she had not told them everything. Yet Nash, concentrating grimly over his iron shot to a par three hole, seemed totally absorbed in the challenges of this infuriating game. But he would not be the first murderer who had successfully compartmentalized the different areas of his life.

And what was the Superintendent in charge of the case to make of George Goodman, the only one of his three companions he had not yet interviewed? At that moment, Lambert would have liked an opinion on that question from someone else. Bert Hook's solid presence and sturdy dismissal of human pretensions would have reassured him, even if the Sergeant had been able to be no more definitive than he felt himself about the part in this business of the oldest of the suspects.

Goodman, leaning on his club at the edge of

161

the green and regarding Nash's contortions over a six-foot putt with benign amusement, seemed perfectly relaxed. After nine holes, he produced a hip-flask and offered it around the four. Sandy Munro, still watching Lambert rather nervously after completing the first half of the course in only one over par, was the only one who refused the whisky, explaining tersely that spirits did not agree with him.

Goodman accepted the refusal with a wide smile and a relaxed shrug, as though acknowledging the eccentricities of his flock with good grace. He examined his golf ball meticulously as they prepared to address the second half of the course, holding it in his surprisingly delicate and immaculately manicured hands. Lambert was reminded ridiculously of a priest with the communion host; he wished Goodman's bent head did not carry such an obviously ecclesiastical hairstyle.

Goodman, the man who had invited Lambert to join the party and thus set up this strange exercise, now presided over it with genial relish, keeping his own game running smoothly while quick to praise excellence in others. He seemed totally calm, totally in control, at peace with himself and the world around him. Lambert looked forward increasingly to interviewing him.

It was Goodman, inevitably, who finished the match on the seventeenth, taking advantage of the final stroke he received to win it for Lambert and himself, despite Munro's immaculate four. The Super-intendent, excusing himself from the ritual of post-match drinks at the nineteenth on the grounds of pressure of work, found himself two pounds better off for his afternoon's efforts.

It was collected from the opposition by Goodman and delivered to his partner as if he were distributing Maundy Money. He was saved from pomposity only by the ineffable impression he created that he was in some way guying himself in all his actions. Perhaps, after all, his whole bearing was an elaborate act, a façade behind which the more ruthless George Goodman operated in watchful safety.

The four of them stood awkwardly for a moment on the path behind the last green, wondering how to take leave of each other and return to the real and more terrible world of murder and retribution. It was Nash who looked back towards the hollow where the corpse had been found and said conventionally, 'It seems incredible on an afternoon like this that someone we know could have lured Guy Harrington out there and battered him to death.'

Lambert studied him carefully for a moment, assessing whether the dead man's employee was testing the extent of police knowledge of the crime. Then he said quietly, 'But he wasn't, you know.' Three faces turned towards him in surprise: whether it was simulated or real he strove to determine. Munro at least knew that the police were aware that the corpse had been moved: Lambert had indicated that to him in their interview. He was a taciturn man, but he would surely have discussed this with the others; unless he had some reason of his own to leave them in the dark.

Lambert pointed out with the air of a man seeking confirmation, 'You and George found him out there, Tony, so you may have deduced something from the lie of the body.' He found himself still using the forenames of the golf course with his companions, perhaps for the last time. How strange were the intricacies of English etiquette! 'In fact, Harrington was trundled out there on a wheelbarrow and dumped without ceremony.'

'But why, Superintendent?' It was George Goodman, with a characteristic sense of decorum, who returned them to the world of criminal investigation by his use of the title.

Lambert chose to prolong the moments in which he could study their reactions by a detailed exposition. 'Perhaps merely to delay the discovery of the crime: any delay tends to spread the network of suspicion more widely. Perhaps in an attempt—in this case largely unsuccessful—to divert suspicion away from the immediate group who had spent the evening with the dead man. Perhaps because whoever moved it thought the original position of the body pointed to a particular person as murderer.'

He paused between each of the three possibilities, pretending to improvise as he spoke, seeking all the time to increase the tension and study the reactions of his companions.

They were interesting. Nash stared at him wide-eyed, possibly overdoing his shock, but perhaps genuinely surprised by a development he had not anticipated. Goodman listened carefully and nodded slowly as he accepted the logic of the Superintendent's arguments, as if he found the matter of absorbing but detached interest: for an instant, Lambert was reminded of the pathologist Cyril Burgess and his enthusiasm for the processes of detection.

But there was no doubt of the most intriguing reaction among the three. Lambert had told Munro that the police knew where Harrington had fallen to his death, but he had not indicated until now that they knew just how the body had been transferred to the course. And he had still not revealed that he was privately certain that it was Munro who had performed that macabre transfer of the corpse at dead of night. But the reaction of the Scotsman to his revelation about the wheelbarrow was the most interesting of all.

Perhaps Sandy Munro was not as practised in dissimulation as his companions. Or perhaps his emotions on hearing the extent of police knowledge were simply more powerful than theirs. Through the three hours of golf his sharp face had generally maintained a dour impenetrability.

Now for a moment he lost control, and it was animated by fear and dread.

CHAPTER SIXTEEN

Within twenty minutes of the end of their golfing partnership, Lambert was interviewing George Goodman. The golf might have been in another life, so quickly was it erased from their consideration.

Goodman seemed anxious to help the transition, as if he recognized as always the demands of decorum. He came to his appointment still in casual clothes, emphasizing that for him questioning was nothing more than an interruption of his holiday activities, which was necessary, but should be accomplished with the minimum of disturbance.

He had changed his sweater: the V-neck olive green woollen he now wore was complemented by a cream shirt and a dark green silk tie, as if he sought a middle road between the formality which would acknowledge the serious procedures of detection and the casual dress which would indicate how unstressed this business was for him. He had washed of course in the short interval since Lambert had left him; his countenance had been polished to a becoming light pink. He looked almost cherubic in the soft sunlight of the late afternoon.

He settled himself comfortably into the armchair opposite Lambert and said, 'Fascinating to be on the other side of the fence for once, Superintendent. I am watching the efforts of your team with interest. Not many magistrates get the chance to see a murder investigation at first hand. I suppose that's just as well!'

If it was meant as a reminder of his JP status, it was lightly done: his interest and enthusiasm seemed quite genuine. Despite the protective shell of middle-class courtesy he had grown around himself, Lambert rather liked the man. Or what he knew of the man: so far Goodman had preserved his privacy from the intrusions of the murder team better than any of the others in his group. Now he said, like a prosperous solicitor attending to a new client, 'What can I do for you, Mr Lambert?'

Bert Hook was less tolerant of Goodman's easy-going panache than his chief. He flicked his notebook ostentatiously to a new page and said firmly, 'You can start by telling us about the discovery of the body.'

'Of course. Well, I rose earlier than is my

167

wont and—'

'Was there a particular reason for that?'

Goodman smiled, resolutely refusing to be ruffled, treating Hook as if he were a young officer new to CID work and anxious to make an impression, rather than the grizzled veteran he strove to present. 'Only that I hadn't slept very well, Sergeant. No doubt you will wish to know the reason for that too. Well, I never sleep as soundly away from home as I do in my own bed these days. No doubt that is one of the less disturbing side-effects of advancing years. And perhaps we had all eaten not wisely but too well on the previous evening.'

'And drunk quite a lot as well, we have gathered.' Goodman's determined calm seemed to be making Hook uncharacteristically aggressive: Lambert had time to wonder if that was the effect the man had intended, so that his own calm might be the more impressive.

'Indeed, as you say, a good deal of wine and the best part of a bottle of brandy had been consumed.' It was the most accurate summary they had been offered: for all his relaxed magnanimity, Goodman had been recording the events of the evening shrewdly. 'I hadn't drunk very much myself, but then I find even a modest amount of alcohol seems to keep me awake nowadays. So your inference may well be correct, Sergeant. Perhaps it was the dehydrating effects of the brandy that prevented me from sleeping very much. At any event, I was awake with the dawn chorus, and I don't think I managed anything more than a few minutes' doze after that.'

'So what time did you get up?' Hook was anxious to record the first fact on his still unsullied page.

'It must have been about six. When I finally accepted that I wasn't going to get any more sleep.'

'And you met Mr Nash at what time?' Hook, happy to see the first figures appearing in his slow, round hand, prepared for a second entry.

Goodman pressed his fingers together and pointed them towards the ceiling. He studied them, appeared to find their symmetry satisfactory, and said, 'It must have been about twenty or twenty-five past six. I'd shaved and made a cup of tea in my room before I caught sight of Tony through the window and stepped forth. It was such a beautiful morning that it tempted me.'

'Had you arranged to meet Mr Nash at that time?'

'Oh no.' For the first time, Goodman's reply was hurried, as if he were anxious to remove any notion of collusion between himself and Tony Nash. His reaction set Lambert thinking. None of the party could have been in bed much before one; Harrington had probably been murdered some time in the hour after that. To find two of them meeting just after six the next morning was a little curious, in the circumstances, especially as Goodman now seemed anxious to establish that the meeting was a chance one. Adapting Wilde, he thought that one person unable to sleep and thus abroad at such a time might be curious, but two suggested collusion.

As if he had caught the thought, Bert Hook said, 'Mr Nash was merely unable to sleep, like you?' He managed to imply in his tone that he didn't believe a word of this.

Goodman was discomposed for the first time. He said, 'There was no rendezvous arranged between us, if that's what you mean. Has anyone suggested there was?'

Hook was too old a campaigner to answer that. When a subject as imperturbable as George Goodman was on the run, you kept him moving. Bert said, 'And after this random meeting, you decided to play golf at that time in the morning?' This time Bert's scepticism was genuine enough: he still could not comprehend why anyone would waste his time on such a ridiculous game when there was serious stuff like cricket to be undertaken. And golf before breakfast at that; it was all highly suspicious.

Goodman, understanding none of the Sergeant's sturdy prejudices, looked suitably puzzled for a moment. 'Yes. I think I suggested it, as a matter of fact. It was a beautiful morning, and the course was completely deserted at that hour.'

He looked automatically to Lambert, no doubt believing that a fellow-golfer would immediately understand. The Superintendent's smile was as much at Hook's sporting bigotry as in acknowledgement of Goodman's mute appeal, but he said, 'An empty course on such a morning would have been an irresistible invitation to me too, George.' With the return to golf, he had dropped automatically back to a first-name address; he caught Hook's stern disapproval. 'Was Tony Nash as keen as you on the idea? He doesn't really strike me as an enthusiast for early morning exercise.'

Goodman smiled. 'No, I agree. But on this occasion he seemed only too anxious for activity.' He thought back: what he had scarcely remarked at the time might now seem significant. 'He looked as if he'd had even less sleep than I had. There were bags under his eyes and his hair was all over the place. And his clothing was all dishevelled, as if it had been thrown on in a hurry. I remember that I got him to tuck his shirt in before we started.' He stopped, as if aware that what had seemed amusing at the time might now be more sinister in the eyes of others.

'Would you say that Tony Nash is normally careless about his dress?'

If Goodman was dissimulating, he did it well. It was with an air of reluctance that he

171

said, 'No. Rather the reverse, I think. I'm no expert on modern fashions, but I'd say he fancied himself as rather a dapper dresser.'

'Did he appear preoccupied when you were on the course?'

Goodman thought carefully, with the air of balancing his loyalty to a friend against his public duty to be as informative as possible to the representatives of the law. 'No. As far as I can remember, we both played reasonably well. Tony smoked more cigarettes than I've ever seen him use before, but he seemed to find the physical activity a release.'

'And you played quite a few holes before you came across the body.'

'Yes. Eleven, to be precise. We'd agreed to play to the twelfth, which you may remember is conveniently near the clubhouse. In fact, we were just completing the eleventh when one of the green staff shouted to us from that hollow where Guy was lying. I suppose, strictly speaking, it was he who found the body, though of course he had no idea who it was.'

Lambert watched Hook's busy ballpoint for a moment, as if waiting for him to catch up with developments. Then he said quietly, 'What was Tony Nash's reaction to the body? Was he as totally surprised as you would expect an innocent man to be?'

Goodman considered the matter carefully. These men would be asking others about his own reactions, no doubt. It was an uneasy thought, which he had not directly considered earlier. He shrugged his episcopal shoulders, inclined the tonsorial head like one unwilling to be uncharitable to anyone, least of all his friend. 'Tony was shocked, as one would expect. As, indeed, I was myself. I was too upset to take much note of whether Tony was behaving naturally. I wouldn't know what naturally is, anyway. I haven't an extensive experience of finding dead bodies.' It was a perfectly valid point, and he knew it. He permitted himself a small, acerbic smile.

Lambert had expected nothing more. But this seemed suddenly an area worth probing; he sensed an unease beneath the comfortable shell of courtesy. 'As I told you earlier, the body had been moved to that spot from the point of the actual murder. I want you to review the moment of discovery now with that knowledge in mind. To put it bluntly, either Tony Nash was as shocked as any innocent person would be to discover the corpse, or he was a murderer pretending a surprise and horror which he did not feel. I can't expect you to distinguish between the two, as you have already indicated. But a murderer might have been surprised to find the corpse in that particular place. Unless he had himself moved the body: at this stage we have an open mind about that possibility. With the benefit of hindsight, can you recall anything in the bearing of Tony Nash which might suggest he was surprised to find the remains of Guy Harrington in that hollow on the course?'

Lambert, even as he put the question, fancied he had set an impossible task: it would surely be impossible to distinguish between two sorts of shock in such circumstances. But if Goodman tried to implicate Nash, that would open up fascinating possibilities, for it might indicate a killer accepting the bait to incriminate someone else. Lambert tried to appear unexcited during a long, almost theatrical pause, while Goodman stared over his head at the wall behind him, apparently in deep and dutiful concentration.

Eventually Goodman sighed and said, 'It's impossible to say, Superintendent. We were both under stress, obviously. Perhaps I didn't even notice Tony's reaction very much—one is overcome by one's own emotions at moments like that. I must say I wasn't too surprised when you told us earlier that Guy's body had been moved from the place where he met his death. I wonder if Tony would say the same thing.'

'We shall find out in due course,' said Lambert with a small, grim smile. 'Are you able to go any further?'

Goodman hesitated; for a moment, Lambert wondered if he was actually enjoying this. 'I think it must have been something about the way the body was lying. With the stomach up in the air and the feet and head sloping down on either side of the mound, I mean. I didn't put the thought into words until you spoke to us about it earlier, but I suppose I thought it was an odd position for anyone to fall into. When you said he had been dumped there, it suddenly seemed to make a lot more sense.'

He had led them elaborately down a cul-de-sac. But it might be perfectly innocent. Goodman had the air of a man clarifying his own thoughts while trying earnestly to help them. Lambert concealed his disappointment with a curt nod to Hook to take up a different, more routine line of questioning. The Sergeant said briskly, 'We need an account of your movements after the party broke up on the night of the murder.'

'Of course. Though I'm afraid it's quite dull. The six of us talked for quite a long time on the roof, as I'm sure the others have told you. That's when I probably had a little too much brandy for my very limited capacity. When we broke up, I went straight back to my room. And so, almost immediately, to bed.'

'Were there any witnesses to this?'

'Regrettably no, Sergeant. Harrington and I had single rooms. The other two couples are no doubt able to speak for each other, but I saw no one after I left the roof until I met Tony Nash next morning.'

Lambert saw no reason to tell him that the two couples involved seemed to be getting

175

themselves into incriminating tangles rather than helping each other. Instead he said abruptly, 'What were your own feelings towards Harrington, Mr Goodman?'

The avuncular features showed no sign of tension; Goodman must have expected that they would come to this. His answer had the ring of a prepared statement. 'We were golfing friends. That is all. You can play golf with a man without approving of him, you know.'

'Indeed I do. Though the association is usually a little closer when one chooses to go away on a golfing holiday with someone.'

'I suppose so. Oh, Guy could be agreeable enough company when he chose to be so. Which I suppose was for most of the time.'

Lambert studied him closely, then said, 'I don't think it will be news to you that Harrington has emerged from our investigation as a thoroughly unlikeable man. You are far too intelligent to have expected anything else. I must ask you to be more specific about your own relationship with him.'

'I didn't like him.' For the first time, Goodman was tight-lipped. The contrast with his previous expansiveness made it quite apparent, to him as to them. He said after a moment, 'I didn't kill him.'

Lambert ignored the lame disclaimer and ventured, 'I believe you hated him, Mr Goodman. Quite enough to wish him dead.'

As he had intended, the man opposite him

made the almost inevitable assumption. 'I suppose the others told you that. All right, I suppose that's fair enough. We got along on the surface, but that was all. I was quite glad when I looked into that hollow near the twelfth and saw him dead.'

'And why did you hate him, Mr Goodman?' Not for the first time, Hook noted the contrast in Lambert's own style, between the esoteric line of inquiry he had tested earlier and the rapid series of more direct questions now.

Goodman was ruffled by the change. 'I—I did some work for him. I'm an architect, you know. An extension to his works. Guy took a long time to pay. We couldn't—'

'Are you saying that you felt strongly enough to wish a man dead over a disagreement about payment?'

Goodman's shoulders, which had earlier shrugged with the control of a mannered gesture, now twitched; Lambert could not be sure whether in anger or despair. 'It sounds odd, I know. But somehow things just went from bad to worse.'

This time it was Lambert who paused, letting the feebleness of this explanation hang between them for a moment. Then he said, 'Harrington had a reputation as an unscrupulous ladies' man, I believe.' He was sure there must be a more direct and brutal modern term.

But the effect on Goodman was startling

177

enough. The blue-grey eyes, so benevolent in the persona he presented successfully to the world around him, widened in resentment. He said unsteadily, 'I believe so. I wouldn't know much about it.'

His whole bearing gave the lie to that. Lambert said, 'Forgive me, Mr Goodman, but this is a murder inquiry. I presume your wife knew Harrington.'

'Yes.'

'For a number of years?'

'Yes.'

'I have to ask you if there was at any time between them a relationship which went beyond mere friendship.'

'Why do you "have to ask"?' Goodman attempted irony, but it came out as almost a snarl.

'Because sexual jealousy is behind a very high percentage of murders.' As Goodman became more disturbed, his interlocutor grew more icily calm.

'Anne never had an affair with Harrington. She hated him as much as I did. Now, are you satisfied?'

Lambert made no attempt to answer a question he took to be rhetorical. Nor to remind Goodman that hatred was a passion not too far removed from love, once love went wrong. Instead he said, 'And what about your own relationship with Mrs Harrington, Mr Goodman?'

Goodman's gasp made even the outwardly impassive Hook look up from his notes. He said, 'I don't have to answer this, you know.'

'Indeed no, Mr Goodman. Your knowledge of the law would tell you that. But as a JP, you would no doubt be anxious to help the police with their inquiries into a serious crime.' Lambert was as bland and assured as Goodman had been when he came into the room.

Goodman made a wretched attempt to recover his former panache. 'That is so, of course. You must forgive me; personal involvement in a murder inquiry seems to upset one's normal standards.' He smoothed his palms unnecessarily down the white fringe of hair at each side of his head. 'Marie Harrington and I have known each other for years. We have been close friends—nothing more. Is that what you wanted to know?'

'She seems to have been well aware of her husband's sexual liaisons. Have you had occasion to consult with or assist her at any time in relation to his various affairs?'

'No.' The monosyllable came too quickly, too vehemently. 'We've known each other for twenty years and more. Through good times and bad. I suppose I may have provided a shoulder to cry on at times. Nothing more. I can't even remember, so it can't be very significant.'

Lambert was intrigued by the manner rather

179

than the content of his replies. Goodman's excitement during their recent exchanges convinced him there was something to be unearthed here, though whether it would prove of relevance to Harrington's death only time would tell. He said, 'Well, I shall need to see Mrs Harrington again.' It sounded like a threat, but that situation was of Goodman's making, not his. 'I must ask you, as you might expect, whether you have any idea who might have killed Guy Harrington.'

Goodman was at ease again, with what to others had seemed the most solemn of questions. 'I'm afraid I haven't. I've thought about it, of course, but I haven't come up with anything useful. I suppose you are still convinced it was one of our group?'

Lambert afforded him a thin smile. 'Convinced would be too strong a word. But we've eliminated a variety of other possibilities, so that it remains the likeliest solution.' He had almost said 'scenario': it must be the effect of late-night reading of criminologist symposium papers. He saw no reason to relay to Goodman the view that Marie Harrington must be added to their group as a leading suspect.

A few minutes later George Goodman sat in the blessed privacy of his own room. His head was in his hands. Presently, he lowered them to grip the arms of his chair, while he stared unblinkingly ahead. To an observer glancing casually through the window, he would have appeared as sleekly self-assured as ever.

But his features showed the strain he could not reveal to the world.

THURSDAY

CHAPTER SEVENTEEN

'Eat some breakfast, John, for goodness' sake!' Christine Lambert watched the toast going cold and hard and knew that it would be left again. The case must be at a difficult stage: it was the only time when her husband forgot to eat.

'Where's the bacon and egg, then?' Lambert snatched up his knife in mock eagerness. It was a running joke between them that she had cut out all his favourite dishes with her campaign against cholesterol.

'I've told you, you can have a grill in the evenings, once a week. Get your toast and marmalade, and drink that tea before it's cold.' She watched him make a dutiful effort, knowing that as soon as she took her eyes off him his mind would be back on the conference he was to hold with his team that morning. In desperation she said, 'I've booked that week in Cyprus at the autumn half-term.'

'Good,' said her husband, with a noticeable lack of enthusiasm. They both knew he would have to be prised away from England when the time came. For the moment, Christine was content to have fed in the news without any violent reaction; at least his preoccupations with the case allowed that. She made her ritual admonition about locking the doors when he left—for a senior policeman he was ludicrously lax about security—and left for school.

Her husband remembered as soon as she had gone that he had forgotten to ask about his daughter's progress. No doubt Christine would have rung Jacqui last night to get the latest progress on the pregnancy, while he was still studying the material accumulating in the murder room at the Wye Castle. Well, no doubt he would have heard the news, if there was any. But he wished he had remembered to ask; twenty-five years of marriage had at least developed that tiny twinge of conscience in him.

It was a rather bleary-eyed Bert Hook that he picked up twenty minutes later. The Open University late night and early morning broadcasting times were taking their toll, even on a student still full of the excitement higher education brings to those who come to it late. 'Now that I'm picking up a student,' said Lambert, 'I expect a "shining morning face".'

'Expect away,' said Hook sourly. 'I look forward to the day when you will cease to give

182

me your selection of "wise saws and modern instances", but I suppose I shall be equally disappointed.'

'I hope all this education isn't going to make you uppity with your elders and betters.' Lambert felt suddenly cheered by the familiarity of his surroundings; trundling the old Vauxhall through the edge of the Cotswolds on a late spring morning with Bert Hook at his side, it seemed that they could not be as far from a solution as he had felt when he rose an hour earlier. There had been a sharp shower just after dawn, but the sun was already climbing against a clear sky and the hawthorn seemed new-washed for their inspection. Nothing evil could triumph on a day like this.

It was a sentimental view, of course: an illusion which later events would comprehensively shatter.

* * *

The detective as individual superman is largely a creation of fiction.

Lambert would be aware by the end of the morning that his team had unearthed at least as much as he had about the participants in the drama that was unfolding at Wye Castle Golf and Country Club. Each man and woman knew the job assigned to them; co-ordinating their discoveries, which was the purpose of this meeting, was a key process in the conduct of a murder inquiry. Each year, the capacity of a Superintendent to act as an intelligent maverick was a little diminished, his importance as a leader of a team a little increased.

In the Murder Room, DI Rushton had already set out the chairs for their meeting. In front of each seat, there were several sheets of blank paper on the edge of the table. For all the world as if they were attending a conference about selling paint, not catching criminals, thought Bert Hook.

The patient accumulation and organization of material by a large group of officers becomes ever more important as technology advances. The importance of routine police work was nowhere better illustrated than in their first subject of discussion that morning. Lambert said, speaking like a committee chairman, 'We'll go through each of our suspects in turn, I think, feeding in the forensic and other evidence as we go along. I've now interviewed all the people in the golfing party of which Harrington was a member, following up the initial statements they gave to members of this team. I have a feeling we need to add one name to these suspects: that of Marie Harrington, the victim's widow. I spoke to her, as most of you know, when she turned up and insisted on identifying the body, but I haven't conducted any formal interview with her, and I don't think anyone else has.' He looked around the table; heads shook in unison.

Rushton said, 'We have the report from the CID in Surrey of her movements on the night of the murder. She was at a dinner with friends, which broke up at about ten-thirty. She had her own car, so that they can't be sure of her movements after that. But she indicated that she was going home.'

'Was she occupying the house on her own?'

'Yes. So she has no witness to her movements until the next morning. The postman says she took the mail from him on the doorstep in her dressing-gown.' He consulted the telex in front of him. 'That was at approximately eight thirty-five.'

'And she must have heard about the death shortly after that.'

'At nine-thirty. The WPC says she took it calmly.'

From what Lambert had seen, that was probably an understatement. He thought of her spare, erect figure, the strong features beneath the impeccably groomed grey hair. And the grey eyes beneath that hair, which had mocked his clumsy attempts at compassion for a grieving widow.

Rushton, saving the most intriguing fact until the end, said, 'There was one interesting thing. The CID sergeant checked with the neighbours. One of them—nosy cow, but probably reliable, he thinks—says she thinks she heard Marie Harrington putting her car in the garage at about two-thirty a.m.'

The men round the table were silent, each occupied with the same arithmetic. Lambert remembered her words 'It's not much over a hundred miles, you know!' in explanation of her unexpected arrival at the Wye Castle. Between ten-thirty and two-thirty, she could have driven to the Wye Castle, thrust her husband over the parapet to his death, and returned home. She would have used the M4 and the A40: good roads, quiet enough at that time of night. Allow her half, perhaps three-quarters of an hour at the hotel; it could have been done that way. And almost without suspicion: without a nosy neighbour, she would not even have been under consideration. Lambert had been thinking of her until now as at most an accessory, not the executioner.

'But why be back here by twelve o'clock the next day?' he said, looking round the table. 'Wouldn't you keep a low profile if you'd got rid of your husband with a ready-made group of suspects around him?'

Unexpectedly, it was Hook who made a suggestion based on a psychological conjecture. 'I don't believe that old rubbish about murderers feeling a compulsion to return to the scene of the crime. But many people who kill are hyperactive, at any rate around the time of the homicide. However ill-advised it may be, they prefer to know what is

186

going on rather than to sit quietly at home wondering whether they've got away with it, waiting for the knock at the door which tells them they've been rumbled.'

Lambert considered the idea. 'She certainly had a strange kind of energy when she arrived here. She was anxious to know whether we were treating the death as a murder, almost pleased when she found we were. And she insisted on identifying the corpse there and then, at the point where we had discovered it.' There were other explanations as well as the one Hook had suggested for Marie Harrington's behaviour on that day, but her actions could scarcely be described as rational, much less normal.

Rushton said, 'She's still in this area. Presumably at the hotel where she told us she'd be staying overnight after she'd identified the corpse.'

Lambert nodded thoughtfully. 'I rather gathered she intended to stay around here until after the inquest. Incidentally, the Coroner plans to open the inquest the day after tomorrow. Do we know whether Marie Harrington has been in touch with any of our five at the Wye Castle?'

It was DI Rushton's moment. 'Indeed she has, sir. I saw it happen, quite by chance. I was in the Cathedral at Hereford on my day off yesterday.' He paused for an instant, as if such behaviour might be thought eccentric enough in a policeman to need explanation. 'I saw her there and watched for a few minutes. She met George Goodman.'

'By chance?'

'I don't think so. She was in the Lady Chapel, and she waited for him to arrive. I'm sure they met by arrangement.'

'Did she see you?'

'No. I'm pretty certain neither of them did. They sat together for a few minutes towards the front of the Chapel. They spoke to each other, but I couldn't catch anything they said. I thought it better not to let them know I was around.' He stopped, recalling that curious moment when the pair had been frozen like a detail from an old master against the stained glass.

'Did they leave the Cathedral together?'

'Yes. I followed them to the car park. They drove away in Goodman's Rover.'

There was a silence round the table. The professionals were recreating the scene, trying to assess its significance. Rushton, who was pleased to display his vigilance even during off-duty time to the chief, wished now that he had rung in yesterday about the incident. In the present silence, it seemed more significant than it had done at the time.

Lambert said, 'Did they appear to be lovers?'

'No. I've thought about that since. They hardly touched each other, as far as I could see. She seemed to put her hand briefly on his when they met, but that was all. I couldn't detect any reaction from him. Perhaps the Cathedral inhibited them: I've no idea how they behaved in the car after they'd driven out of the city.' It was the policeman's automatic caveat, coming from the early years they had all endured of flashing torches into darkened cars while patrolling the beat.

Of course, thought Lambert, people still had occasion to meet after affairs had run cold. There was no saying that the magisterial Goodman and the elegant widow Harrington had not consorted together more hotly in the past. But it was of interest only if it bore on the events of the last few days. He said, 'I shall need to see Marie Harrington again. It will be interesting to see if she confesses to yesterday's meeting. I interviewed Goodman yesterday afternoon, and he said nothing about it, though I broached his relationship with Marie Harrington with him directly. Interesting . . . Right: let's move on to the Munros.'

It was Rushton as Deputy who had assumed the role of the marshaller of various findings. 'The most interesting thing we've come up with is the forensic material. Harrington died almost instantaneously after a fall on to the gravel path from the roof where the group had been drinking earlier: a height of something over sixty feet. There is worsted from his trousers on the edge of the parapet. He was certainly dead before he was moved.'

Automatically, he was rehearsing the details which would be necessary for the Coroner to 'open' the inquest and adjourn it under Section 20 of the Coroners' Acts. It would be a five-minute process, but all these facts would have to stand up eventually to examination by a Defence Counsel in the High Court; the team were patient with him through his mental checking of their work, hearing it transformed through his calm tones into evidence.

'The body was moved in the wheelbarrow? We're certain of that?'

'Yes. There are fibres from the back of Harrington's jacket on the front of the barrow above the wheel, and from the back of his trouser legs on the bit between the shafts. It won't be important, but if we had to we could establish the position of the body in the barrow while it was being transported.'

They were silent, picturing Harrington's last journey at dead of night, the corpse still warm, the head and feet dancing with each movement of the single wheel over the uneven earth. Lambert moved to the aspect of that journey that really excited them as detectives. 'And the fibres from what we think is Munro's sweater. Where exactly were they found?'

'On the body. On the back of the jacket, to either side of Harrington's shoulder-blades, on the backs of his trousers, and on the heel of one of the shoes. We'll need the sweater, of course, but once we have it, Forensic are quite confident their evidence will stand up in court.'

'It may not need to. I'm seeing Munro after we've finished here. I'll get the sweater from him then. I doubt whether he'll hold out against evidence like that: I don't see him denying that he moved the body. Are there any prints?'

Rushton looked down at the forensic report, checking a detail he did not quite understand. 'None, sir. The left hand was gloved: the right wasn't, but he seems to have wrapped something round it—possibly a handkerchief or a piece of towelling, they think in the labs. Seems odd that a man should wear one glove.'

Lambert smiled. 'Not to a golfer it doesn't. Munro has played for forty years. Probably he had a golfing glove in the pocket of the trousers he was wearing when he moved the body. Golf gloves are only worn singly, on the left hand in the case of a right-handed player. He must have put on the clothes he had worn earlier in the day for golf to move the body: he wasn't wearing the sweater during the evening.'

'Things look pretty black for Munro, then.' This was Sergeant Johnson, the uniformed man who headed the Scene of Crime team. He brightened at the thought that they were near to an arrest; his weekend's fishing might yet be saved.

Lambert weighed the matter. 'At the moment they do, yes. I've little doubt that he moved that body—I don't go very much on the idea of someone else wearing his sweater to incriminate him, though we've all known stranger things. The fact that he moved the body doesn't automatically mean that he killed Harrington, of course. But he lied to me when I interviewed him. Clumsily. Whether he was trying to protect himself, his wife or some third party I hope to find out when I see him.'

'What about Mrs Munro?' said Rushton. He had taken the initial statement from the striking, dark-haired Alison himself, and found it hard going.

'She told us that her husband was in bed and probably asleep when she got back to the room on the night of the murder. That, I think, was a lie, but we shall know for certain before long. She'll have compared notes with her husband, and be aware that their stories conflict. There's something else too. Bert, would you read out her exact words about what she did on that night after the party broke up and left the roof, please?'

Hook flicked over a page. 'She said, "I wandered round for a little while before going to bed. Perhaps we'd all drunk a little too much."'

'Pretty lame, you'll agree,' said Lambert. 'We let her get away with it because I was anxious to see what she had to say about her husband. And because I knew I had other people to see who might give me more information about Alison Munro's movements in that crucial twenty minutes. Sure enough, we had an interesting contribution from Meg Peters. She says that Alison Munro went back to the roof garden; that she heard her having what she called "a hell of a row" with Harrington after Tony Nash had left him.'

There was silence round the table: it was the first most of them had heard of this. Then Rushton said, 'It may be that Meg Peters herself is not a reliable witness. She's the only one of our suspects with a record.'

'I know that, Chris.' Lambert was pleased with himself for using Rushton's first name, he thought quite deftly. 'We'll need to sort out the truth of the matter very carefully. But if what Meg Peters says is true, Alison Munro was the last person we know of to date who was with Harrington; and she was quarrelling with him.'

There was silence around the table. All these men had a clear picture of Alison Munro's dark hair and strong, English beauty. He fancied that none of them until this moment had seriously entertained her as their murderer. He said, 'What about Tony Nash?'

Rushton said, 'We haven't turned up a lot that's new about him. Except that he made no secret of his hatred of Harrington over these last months, even at work. Not the wisest of tactics to go round slagging off the boss, I'd have thought, and Nash never did it until recently. But he's been virulent about it since about Easter; even taken to saying things about getting even with him, apparently.'

Lambert could see Nash as a choleric man, but the decline in control in recent weeks was interesting. 'Anything else?'

'Yes. One small but interesting fact. Nash wasn't originally in the party to come here this week. Someone else dropped out and he almost forced his way in. The others were glad enough to have him, but worried that his vehement hatred of Harrington might surface and destroy the party. But they say he was determined to come.'

'Determined to have the opportunity to get at Harrington, do you think? It's possible. Munro says that Harrington himself came into the party late, which means that Nash may have joined the group only after he learned his boss was to be part of it. They quarrelled openly on the evening of the murder, and according to George Goodman, Nash was abroad early on the morning after, looking thoroughly disturbed and dishevelled. According to the others, he isn't habitually an early riser, but on that morning he was out before half past six.' Lambert was gratified to see Rushton looking puzzled. 'I discovered that in my formal interview with Goodman late yesterday afternoon. After I had unearthed various interesting details of our suspects' habits in the more informal context of the golf course yesterday,' he explained loftily to the table at large. Rushton's deadpan face gave nothing away; he thought eccentric was a polite epithet for a superintendent who played golf with the leading suspects in a murder investigation, but he was too well versed in the rule-book to reveal his disapproval in front of subordinates. He said, 'What did you make of George Goodman, sir?'

Lambert smiled. He had been wondering exactly what he made of George Goodman ever since the conclusion of his interview with him on the previous day. 'That he isn't the self-satisfied bourgeois he pretends to be. But exactly what he is, I'm not sure. His account of the period when Harrington was murdered has no witness. But, as he said with considered naïvety himself, as he occupies a single room here, we could hardly expect a convenient demonstration of his innocence. There is more to Mr Goodman than he cares to reveal, I'm quite sure, but whether that more includes a man capable of violent murder, I'm not yet certain.' He looked round the table. 'What have your various researches turned up?'

Rushton looked a little impatiently at the typewritten summary in front of him. He had some decidedly interesting material to reveal, but not about George Goodman. 'Not much. No obvious close connections with the victim. He didn't have a working association, like

Nash and Munro. He did occasional small planning jobs for Harrington—works extensions and the like. Harrington seems to have been slow to pay on a couple of occasions, but there is no evidence that they fell out seriously about it. There is a minimum of correspondence in Harrington's files about it.'

'You're sure there's no real acrimony? Goodman claimed when I spoke to him yesterday that there was. He admitted to real ill-feeling between himself and Harrington, and gave a dispute over plans he had drawn for Goodman as the cause. It didn't seem a very strong reason at the time.'

'No trace in writing of any bust-up between the two. Of course, there has been no access to Goodman's files. But no one at Harrington's factory suggested there'd been any argument over the architectural work that Goodman did for Harrington.'

'Was there anything more personal, then? Had Harrington got his paws on Goodman's wife? Or even Goodman on Harrington's—I'm sure there's a spot or two of the old Adam beneath that saintly exterior.'

Rushton frowned at the sheet in front of him. He was less happy with speculations about emotional attachments than with the clear facts of contracts and money. 'Nothing that we've been able to turn up. Harrington had a go at lots of women, including our Miss

Peters, but—'

'Did Mrs Goodman ever work for him?'

'No. She hasn't worked anywhere except in her husband's office since they were married thirty years ago.'

'What about Marie Harrington? Did you dig up any associations between her and Goodman?'

'Only of the kind that are probably quite innocent. They've known each other for twenty years, but the kind of social exchange they've had has mostly involved Mrs Goodman as well. Of course, most of what I'm reporting has been gathered by CID in Surrey, so in that sense it's second-hand information.'

Lambert heard Rushton making the reservation without rancour; at the same age, he might well have done it himself. It was the old detective's nightmare of overlooking some key factor that would later seem obvious to all, the obsessive need to check the authenticity of every piece of information before it became part of the framework of the case.

It looked as if the picture of Goodman's happy, unexceptional family life was proof against the diggings of a team trained to be sceptical about such things. The probing of the surface tissue of his existence had produced nothing that was not benign. Whether because he wanted to round off this family unit of Trollopean simplicity, or because he was unable to accept Goodman's portrait of himself without a final check, he said, 'Have the Goodmans any children?'

Rushton was glad to be prompted towards a demonstration of the thoroughness of his documentation; he wished now he had not just reminded the chief that most of the work had been done by another force. 'Two. The elder is a boy. Qualified now as a solicitor, working up in Cheshire. The other is a girl.' He looked down at the telex; information had come in thick and fast, so that he hadn't been able to analyse it as he liked to do. Perhaps after all he shouldn't have taken his day off this week. 'Privately educated, didn't go on to higher education like her brother. Actually worked for Harrington's firm for about a year.' He paused: it was the first time he had seen this.

'How long ago?' Lambert's tone was studiously neutral. No point in bawling anyone out: this was no more than one fact in a plethora of information that had to be sifted and organized. Probably, in any case, it meant no more than any one of a hundred others.

'Two years. She left of her own accord, apparently. She seems to have been no more than a junior employee.' Rushton turned over a sheet. 'I don't think anyone in Surrey has actually interviewed Mrs Goodman. Or the daughter herself, for that matter. Do you want me to organize it?'

'No. I'll go over there myself if necessary. It needs someone who can put things together with what's happening here. If we don't get to the root of this in the next two days, there may be several people we need to see over there.' There was silence around the table, as they reviewed the depressing prospect of the net widening, of routine leg-work over a wider area, taking in ever more people, following leads that seemed ever less likely. All of them knew that most of those murders unsolved after a week remained unsolved, however long the files stayed officially open.

Rushton said, 'We've been able to come up with rather more on Meg Peters than on Goodman—or anyone else, for that matter.'

There was a stirring of interest around the table: Ms Peters was the most striking and memorable face among the group who had surrounded Guy Harrington. Scandal attaching to glamour has an additional flavour, and policemen, chauvinist or otherwise, are human, despite some contemporary opinion.

Rushton said, 'The conviction for cannabis possession you already knew about, sir. But two years after that there was another court appearance, though not in the dock. A company called Abbeydale Films was prosecuted for making and selling obscene material: blue films. Usual sort of thing—bedroom romps which were too explicit to be ignored once a few complaints came in. A grubby little company by the sound of it, and a fairly routine case. But they made the mistake of pleading not guilty. Which meant that witnesses were called by the prosecution. Three men and a girl. The girl was one Margaret Eileen Peters. No photographs, lads, unfortunately.'

'Meg Peters wasn't charged with anything?'

'No. She appeared in court for perhaps two minutes, by the sound of it. Gave evidence that she'd performed what was required of her under direction, rather than contributed any improvisations of her own. It was twelve years ago.'

'Did you find any overt connection with this case?'

'No. The company was prosecuted and went out of business. Or changed its name and found another place to operate.'

Lambert frowned, pondering the unanswerable question: had this titillating bit of information anything to do with a murder committed twelve years later? Or should it be consigned with the other ninety-five per cent of CID research to the tray marked irrelevant? Any detective who could spot that right five per cent quickly was assured of long-term success. 'Any suggestion from your work on the dead man that he knew about Meg Peters's work in blue films?'

'No, sir. But we'd be lucky if that showed up anywhere on paper. And we haven't had the chance to question anyone about it; the information only came through this morning.'

'I'll see Miss Peters myself. Harrington knew about her drugs conviction. It will be interesting to know whether he knew about this. And whether anyone else in the group who came here this week knew.'

Lambert adjourned the conference once he ascertained none of the group had any more ideas to float. It had run longer than he planned, and left him with much to do. He didn't mind that: it was to point the way forward that such meetings were held. The Munros had to be challenged about several issues, particularly Sandy's moving of the body. The small but possibly significant connection of Goodman's daughter with the dead man had to be checked out.

Nash's determination to be here this week, when he was not in the original party, needed to be investigated, alongside his perturbed state on the morning after the murder. So did Meg Peters's participation in an unsavoury industry, and whether any or all of the golfing party knew of it. He needed to be clear about Marie Harrington's possible involvement in the murder, and her views on several of the other issues now raised. He paused for thought there: he had the feeling that the cool and unconventional widow of the victim might be the catalyst in the final stages of this investigation.

He was being drawn towards a late lunch by a resolute Bert Hook when the phone rang.

'Chief Constable for you, Superintendent,' said the DC who took the call on the murder room line, suitably awed by the voice of divinity.

The CC was as urbane as ever, and as difficult to turn aside from the course he had determined for his staff. 'I've arranged a press conference for four o'clock in Gloucester,' he said. 'I need you there, John. I've held them off as long as I could. We need the PR. They're making my life hell about those child abductions. We need a—a diversion. Yes, I admit it.'

'But, sir, this case is just—'

'No buts, John. Your cases are always at a crucial stage when there is any interruption. We have to carry the public with us and this is part of it. Bring young Rushton with you. He's always good at telling them about the labours of Hercules that go on behind the scenes. Not many of them print it, I know, but it impresses them with the work being done and keeps them off our backs.'

'I can't keep my leading suspects here much longer, sir. Perhaps one more night is as much—'

'Sorry, John, we must have you. Surrey isn't a million miles away, if they do have to leave the scene of the crime.' He sounded curiously like Marie Harrington, the intelligent, sardonic woman he had been planning to see that afternoon.

Then the CC went on inexorably, 'I think the TV cameras for Central South will probably be there.' In the face of such a media presence, Lambert knew further argument was useless.

CHAPTER EIGHTEEN

A mile away from the Wye Castle, Marie Harrington was becoming tired of her hotel room.

It was neat, clean, characterless and claustrophobic. In the confined space, the matching Laura Ashley bedspread and curtains seemed increasingly twee. The en suite bathroom was a useful contribution to privacy, but the conversion had made the bedroom even smaller. The steady drip of the tap into the tiny washbasin, which for two days she had scarcely noticed, seemed unnaturally loud in the quiet of the warm afternoon.

She fancied she was the only one in this area of the hotel. The overnight businessmen had long departed, the tourists were making the most of the unbroken sun, the hotel staff had cleaned the rooms and changed the sheets during the morning. She listened, until the silence seemed a tangible thing, surrounding her, awaiting with interest her next move.

Quiet as the grave, they said. It was an

unfortunate simile for a widow who had not yet buried her husband. Even for a widow who welcomed this death as unequivocally as she did. She had not wavered in that at least. Not even a fleeting nostalgia for old and better times had diluted her relief in the days after Guy's death. There had not been many good moments, even in the first years of their marriage, and any regret for their passing had been exhausted long before her husband's death.

Increasingly, though, she wondered about her determination to stay here until after the inquest, to see the remains of her husband burned before she resumed and developed the life his death had interrupted. There was something superstitious in her resolve to suspend that new life until the formalities of the one with her husband were officially concluded. She was aware of that, but once she had determined upon a course of action she was not easily diverted from it.

Certainly not by a little boredom, she told herself firmly. She addressed herself again to her book, though she had not turned a page for twenty minutes. Nor did she now. Against her wishes, her thoughts turned again to her husband's killer. She had certainly not come here to unmask a murderer, she told herself. For a while she had thought she did not even want to know; then a natural honesty had made her acknowledge that something, perhaps little more than curiosity, had impelled her towards the knowledge she now held.

For she was sure she had determined the identity of her husband's murderer. Her conversation with George Goodman had confirmed her suspicion, though she was not sure whether he was aware of that. He had seemed too preoccupied with his own problems to be conscious of what he revealed about himself and others to a woman listening closely and making her own deductions. But she half-wished she had not asked him to meet her in the Cathedral; the knowledge she now had seemed more and more a burden.

She would not reveal her secret; and not only because the killer had rendered her a welcome service. There had been good reason for this death: in the murderer's shoes, she might well have taken the same opportunity. Now she was relieved of the temptation and grateful to her deliverer. As far as she was concerned, the death could remain the work of a person or persons unknown.

It was the third time that afternoon she had told herself that. She returned to thoughts of the life which her awaited her back in Surrey. She was not sure how seriously involved she was with the man who was her lover. Or how much more seriously she might wish to become involved, in these new circumstances: death altered everything. It was a dilemma she found not unpleasant, though like other things in her new life she was trying to postpone consideration of it until Guy was finally and officially dispatched.

Perhaps in that quiet room she was more on edge than she knew, or admitted to herself. For when the knock came at the door, she started so much that her book leapt from her lap to the carpet. She checked her hair automatically in the mirror of the small dressing-table as she went to the door. The strain in the face she chose not to see.

She did not recognize the figure which almost filled the doorway. A stolid figure, with blue, observant eyes. Powerful shoulders, large, flat hands, waist thickening a little with early middle age. Observant, wary, courteously careful in his attempts not to threaten a woman on her own. He said awkwardly, 'My name is Hook. Sergeant Hook, of the CID. We met briefly at the Wye Castle, when you spoke to Superintendent Lambert on the day of your husband's death.' His careful delivery had the soft, warm vowels of Gloucestershire.

She said, 'I remember you now. I didn't at first. Please come in.'

He came awkwardly into the room, his eyes studiously avoiding the bed which dominated its small floor area, as if by acknowledging it he would be hinting at intimacies beyond his brief. She indicated the room's single armchair and perched herself adroitly on the stool by the dressing-table. It was a small armchair, and he parked himself uneasily on the edge of it. She thought he looked like a newly appointed school prefect coming for the first time into the headmaster's study.

'I really only want to arrange for Superintendent Lambert to see you. Only the phone was out of order, see. I tried three or four times. They said you were out.'

'I'm afraid I told the hotel switchboard to say that, Sergeant. So that I wouldn't be disturbed.' She almost added the 'see' that he had attached to his explanations; the habit was catching, and she had an idea that he was deliberately playing up the countryman in himself. Perhaps he wanted her to think him less acute than he was. 'I wasn't anticipating anything as grand as a CID visit, I must confess.'

'It's Mr Lambert who needs to see you, really. I wouldn't have come at all if I could have arranged it on the phone.'

'No. I'm sorry about that. Well, when would the great man like to see me?'

'Tomorrow morning. First thing, if possible.' Visions of flimsy nightwear flashed before Bert's suggestible eyes, and he said hastily, 'That's to say, just after breakfast. About half past nine?'

'Nine-thirty would be fine, Sergeant. May I ask what is the line of these mysterious inquiries?'

The grey, humorous eyes teased Hook, as if they appreciated immediately his dilemma. If he could find out anything useful today, the chief would be only too pleased; Lambert was the least sensitive of men when it came to the protocol of an investigation. But since he had expected merely to make a telephone appointment for the morrow, he had not thought out his approach for an interview. He said, 'I think he wanted to know a little more about your husband's factory and those he employed. But I'm sure—'

'Any particular employees, Sergeant? I am only too anxious to help the police in the course of their inquiries, you see.' With her use of the cliché, she was gently mocking him, and both of them knew it.

Bert decided she was having things rather too much her own way. His air of cosy rusticity dropped away as he said, 'Mr Nash, for a start. I believe he didn't like your husband, and didn't choose to disguise the fact over the last few months.'

'I've heard reports to that effect, yes. Not many people liked Guy. I don't know why Tony Nash should have grown so open about it recently.'

He waited, feeling she knew at least a little more, but she did not enlarge on the matter. Lambert would press her harder the next day, he felt sure. He said, 'Mr Munro worked for your husband, as well. Was he happy doing

208

so?'

'No.' She smiled at him openly. 'Sandy Munro is a poppet, Sergeant. Perhaps that's not the expression you would use, but accept my word for it.' She was smiling at him now, teasing him openly. 'But he isn't the most forthcoming of men, as perhaps you've found by now. He's got a nice wife: perhaps you could get something out of her. But I mustn't try to teach you your job.' Her smile was wide and empty; Bert remembered similar expressions on stonewallers who had frustrated him for hours at cricket.

'What about Mr Goodman?'

For a moment she looked blank; perhaps she had expected to be pursued harder on the Munros. 'He didn't work for Guy. He's an architect with his own practice. I think he did occasional work when it was commissioned, but they didn't fall out about it. As far as I know.'

'What about Mr Goodman's daughter. Didn't she work for Guy?'

'Did she? It could only have been for a short time. Of course, Guy's was quite a big works, employing about three hundred people in all.'

'You didn't know about her working there?'

'I'm afraid I didn't, Sergeant. Is it important?' Her smile was blander than ever.

'Probably not. In which case, can you tell us anything about Miss Peters which might be of relevance?' Bert was quite pleased with the result of his abrupt transfer to a different subject. Marie Harrington's smile disappeared abruptly and she looked at him sharply; it was the effect he looked for from the ball he reserved for stonewallers, dug in a little short and delivered with extra pace. For a moment, the woman opposite him looked agreeably like a batsman who has seen a ball whistle past his nose.

Then she said, 'She was one of Guy's women. I expect you have discovered that. I'm not sure I can tell you a lot more.'

'She is going to marry Mr Nash.'

'So I understand. I hope they will be very happy.' She was annoyed with herself: the little ironic barb was her first unguarded moment. 'I don't think I can tell you any more about the handsome Meg Peters, Sergeant. As to whether Tony Nash resents her past, you are no doubt closer to that situation than I am.'

Hook said, 'Did you resent Meg Peters yourself, Mrs Harrington?' He had met a succession of smartly dressed, slightly patronizing women among the governors of the Barnardo's homes where he had been brought up. Thinking of Marie Harrington as one of these might be unfair, but it enabled him to be brusque: he had a few scores to settle with the breed.

If his aim was to rattle her, he was successful, briefly. She said, 'That is hardly your business.'

'Not unless it is relevant to a murder inquiry, Mrs Harrington.'

'That, I assure you, it is not. I had learned to pity rather than envy Guy's women a long time before Meg Peters.'

Hook paused, meeting her gaze. Both of them could hear that irritating tap dripping a few yards away. He said quietly, 'You will appreciate on reflection that we cannot accept anyone's assurances at the moment . . . Can you tell me about your own movements on the night of your husband's death, please, Mrs Harrington?'

He had taken her by surprise this time, quite certainly. The fast yorker following the short-pitched ball, catching the opposition on the back foot. She said, 'If you like. I went out to dinner with friends in Camberley. No doubt they can confirm that, if you need to be convinced.' Her asperity signalled a small victory for him in their exchanges.

'And the group broke up at what time?'

'Quite early. I suppose about ten-thirty.'

'And did you then return to your home?'

'Sergeant Hook, what is the point of this?'

'In cases of homicide, it is routine police practice to check the whereabouts of those closest to the deceased. The more people we can eliminate from the inquiry, the greater the resources we can bring to bear on the people who might have committed the crime.'

It was efficiently deadpan, as it should have

211

been. He had explained the position often enough before, to less intelligent and cooperative women than Marie Harrington. She looked at him curiously, weighing the comfortable village-bobby exterior, deciding it was a convenient disguise. Then she said, 'I spent the evening with seven friends, then went home to a cold and celibate bed. I could not possibly have killed Guy. Have you any justification for this line of questioning?'

Hook was wondering how he had got in so deep; he had intended when he came merely to follow Lambert's instructions and arrange a meeting for the morrow. He decided there was no point in suspending operations at this point. 'We have a witness who thinks you did not return to your house until around two-thirty a.m.'

The woman in front of him did not gasp or protest. The large grey eyes widened, and for several seconds she said nothing. Perhaps she was doing the same arithmetic the police had conducted about journey times between Camberley and the Wye Castle; perhaps she was speculating about the identity of their informant. Hook had carefully avoided revealing the sex of the neighbour, but something told him Marie Harrington would be able to make an accurate guess in the matter.

Eventually she said, 'And you think that in that time I might have driven to Herefordshire and killed my husband? It's possible, I suppose, in theory.' She mused for a moment, then took a decision. 'I was with a man. A man I may wish to marry when all this is over. I don't wish to give you his name: for reasons I won't go into now, it would embarrass both of us. But if I have to, I will.'

Hook thought he had gone far enough for the moment. 'That will be up to Superintendent Lambert. We may need to check out the story, to eliminate you from our inquiries. If it has no bearing on the case, there is no reason why the information should not remain confidential.' It was another of his prepared formulae. He stood up stiffly and launched into another, valedictory one. 'Well, I won't take up any more of your time for the present, Mrs Harrington. I shall probably return with Superintendent Lambert to see you in the morning. Unless you would prefer to come to see us? We have set up a Murder Room at the Wye Castle.'

'Here will be fine, thank you, Sergeant. I'm not sure that it is an appropriate sentiment in the circumstances, but you may tell Mr Lambert that I look forward to the renewal of our acquaintance.' She had recovered her poise at the last, just as Hook departed with a resumption of his awkwardness, manoevring his large frame through the scanty spaces between bed, stool and chair as if he were in a doll's house.

When he had gone, the woman he had questioned sat for a while in the chair he had lately occupied, her book unopened on her knee. Surely they couldn't really think she had killed Guy? That would be ironic indeed, when she could tell them if she chose where to look for their killer.

Had she given this Sergeant who was so much shrewder than he chose to appear any clue to the identity of that killer? She didn't think so. She was glad he had mentioned all the people in the group at the Wye Castle, so that she had been blankly unable to help on each one, with a sort of negative neutrality. Had she had Bert Hook's background, she would no doubt have congratulated herself on playing a consistently straight bat.

She was startled when the phone rang, for the first time during her stay. The sturdy Sergeant Hook must have attended to the switchboard operator: she did not look the kind of girl who would be proof against police disapproval. She knew the voice immediately. 'We need to meet,' it said.

'Why?'

'Things to be sorted out. We need to be clear about the story.'

She didn't like that 'we'. She was not part of a conspiracy. Except of silence. 'You needn't worry. I know nothing. I can make informed guesses, but they will go no further.'

'There are things I have to get straight for

214

myself. I shan't contact you again. We'll go our separate ways, once the heat is off.'

The voice was nervous; not as she was used to hearing it. She felt a sudden sympathy, a rush of gratitude for the deliverance the speaker had brought her. 'All right. Tomorrow? It will have to be late morning or afternoon: I have to see Lambert first thing after breakfast.' Leaning to untangle the cord of the phone, she glanced into the mirror, and was surprised to see the tension in her face.

The voice said, 'No. I can't do tomorrow. I'll be seeing Lambert myself. I don't know when yet. Make it tonight.'

Suddenly she too wanted this meeting over quickly. It was part of the business of ridding herself of Guy. 'All right. Here?'

'No. We shouldn't be seen together. You mustn't be implicated. By the river. Just below the Wye Castle: I can't be away from here for long without it being noticed.'

It was true, she supposed. She could see that. Absurdly, she wanted to say how grateful she was. Instead, she said, 'All right. What time?'

'Say ten-thirty. If we should be all together here, I can sneak out at about the time when the bar is shutting. It shouldn't take long.'

They arranged the exact spot. It was no more than ten minutes' walk from her hotel, so that she need not take her car. The less notice she attracted to her movements, the better. No one wanted her accused of complicity.

She put down the phone and stared at it for a long moment. For the first time, she acknowledged to herself that she was feeling the strain. She would be glad after all to have this business over.

CHAPTER NINETEEN

It was hot under the television lights: too hot. And the platform party had been sitting under them for too long.

Lambert, glancing sideways at the beads of sweat on his Chief Constable's face, wondered for a moment if the young producer had roasted them deliberately, setting them up for a confrontation in which their mental discomfort might be expected to follow hard upon the physical. Watching senior policemen squirm seemed very much to the public taste nowadays. A trendy young current affairs producer (did they still call them that?) would no doubt engineer confrontation rather than consensus.

On the whole, Lambert conceded reluctantly, Douglas Gibson was not a bad Chief Constable to work for. He had known a few, and judged by the Superintendent's twin criteria of not interfering with an officer who had his teeth into a case and supporting his force against the pressures of the ignorant, Gibson came out pretty well. In Lambert's view, he had an exaggerated respect for the media and their operatives, and a determined concern to steer a non-controversial course in the last years of his journey towards a pension. But these were characteristics of the modern breed one had to accept, sometimes even welcome.

Lambert had an intrusive remembrance of his first CC in a northern city, who had expected unswerving industry from his men and snarled like a police Alsatian at any newspaper hack unwise enough to come within his sight. It wouldn't do now, said the wise men who appointed Chief Constables. Probably they were right, but Lambert wished fleetingly that the man he was thinking of, now long dead, could be here for a moment to growl his derision.

Gibson defended his main concern, the investigation into the child abductions on the edges of Cheltenham, with deadpan expertise. The massive police presence and frenetic activity which characterized cases of child disappearance had so far drawn an ominous series of blanks, but only the most experienced listeners would have deduced as much from his brisk account of progress. He gave detailed statistics of the numbers of police involved, the painstaking sweeps of difficult woodland ground, the welcome and pleasing cooperation of the public. The younger reporters, many of whom did not specialize in crime, wrote industriously, while their informant studiously refused to catch the eyes of the older hands.

When some of them questioned him insistently about the nearness of an arrest, Gibson gave them the arch half-smile of a man who knows more than he cares to reveal, and spoke of the need for secrecy 'at this delicate stage of the investigation'. Only the officers beside him on the press conference platform knew how worried he was about the lack of anything like a lead.

Nor would he entertain any suggestion that the police were less than dynamic in their pursuit. Twice he resorted to a grim, 'These men will be brought to justice' and struck a granite pose against anyone who might challenge such certainties. When asked why the officer in charge of the investigation was not here to answer questions of detail in person, Gibson said with a hint of acerbic outrage that he was sure the public would rather he was out leading the search for brutal perverts than sitting in the comfort of a city hotel talking about it.

Lambert wondered where that left him. He did not have long to ponder the question, for Gibson brought the questions on the child abductions to an abrupt halt by transferring attention to the murder at the Wye Castle. He introduced Lambert with the flourish of a

218

magician producing a rabbit from a hat, contriving to look a little disappointed when the move brought no applause.

Lambert had been wondering what would happen if he announced that he had had to suspend his investigation at what was genuinely 'a delicate stage' to come and answer questions to which he could give no useful answers, but it was no more than a beguiling vision. Like all visions, it faded abruptly with the intrusion of reality.

The media had come a little belatedly to the idea of homicide at the Wye Castle, having been distracted by lurid disclosures of homosexual rings among Westminster MPs as well as the disappearance of the children. Lambert had to correct the hopeful delusions that Guy Harrington had been bludgeoned to death with a baseball bat, that the corpse had been an unrecognizable mass of blood and gore, that the head had been found some time after the body. He confirmed reluctantly that although Harrington had fallen to his death, foul play was now definitely suspected.

At this point Douglas Gibson intervened. 'Without revealing too much,' he said benignly, 'I think I can say that in this case we feel hopeful of an early arrest.' His eyebrows curved a question at Lambert, with what might have been archness in someone other than a Chief Constable.

Lambert became uncomfortably conscious

219

of the quiet whirr of the television videotape, of the cameraman zooming in on his sweating visage. For a moment he wished he had not waved away the make-up girl and her powder so airily half an hour earlier. When he replied carefully that routine police procedures had narrowed the field of suspects, Gibson smiled like a headmaster endorsing a favourite pupil and said, 'Superintendent Lambert is naturally cautious, a quality of which I thoroughly approve.'

One of the tabloid reporters wanted to know if women figured among the suspects, and the sports reporter of the *Oldford Advertiser*, an aged Welshman called Williams whom Lambert had known for years, began an ironic commentary on the headlines he foresaw. 'Leading industrialist struck down in love nest,' he intoned with relish. Williams resented being transferred from his sporting interests to act for the day as crime reporter: now he scented a little fun.

He was sitting not three yards from Lambert on the front row, and his comments, delivered towards the ceiling with the air of a philosopher, were plainly intended for the Superintendent's amusement. Lambert's heart sank as his practised eye detected the traces of a happy and characteristic inebriation.

'Two women, you say, Mr Lambert,' said another London man, not looking up from his scribblings. 'Are both of them suspects?'

'Saucy sex romps topple tycoon!' muttered Williams reminiscently, his smile recalling long-gone Fleet Street days with fond indulgence.

'Do I understand only one of the women in the party was a wife?' came next from the persistent group at the back of the room, who were now more animated than at any time during the conference.

They were too far back to hear any of Williams's unofficial glosses on their questions. 'Wild orgy goes wrong at plush club,' the Celtic oracle now interpreted. 'The *Sun* doesn't like more than one syllable at a time,' he explained apologetically. Lambert was cheered by the sight of the young producer, who had emerged with arms flapping from his control box. He was directing a variety of minions in search of the invisible source of these disturbing asides, which were in danger of ruining his recording.

One of the tabloid group had plainly done some research. Warming to his task, he shot at Lambert, 'Has this red-haired actress been cleared of suspicion yet, Superintendent Lambert?'

Williams took his attention from the ceiling and fixed the platform party with a single wild eye. 'Titful temptress topples top tycoon,' he said. Overcome with his artistry and the visions it produced in one of his imaginative temperament, he slid slowly down his leather chair and shut that disturbing eye; a beatific smile suffused the whole of his thoroughly lived-in visage.

*   *   *

'They cut you off before you even got into your stride,' said Christine Lambert resentfully as the local news faded to a weatherman lugubriously predicting a continuation of the fine spell. She was more enthusiastic about her husband's occasional television appearances than he was himself, though Lambert had observed the item surreptitiously over the newspaper he had apparently found so absorbing.

'There was more than that in the can,' he said, using the only piece of film jargon he knew with the confidence of a professional broadcaster, 'but it had to be edited.'

'I expect you mumbled as usual,' said his wife.

Lambert reflected that the man who said that no man is a hero to his valet had obviously not been married. 'On the contrary, I was a model of elocution,' he said, with the determined dignity of the liar who knows he cannot be disproved. 'In fact, it was old Williams who had to be edited out. He was making tabloid headlines out of the questions I got. It's a hobby of his.'

'The old boy I met from the *Oldford*
222

Advertiser? He won't get into trouble, will he?' Christine, who had once found a boring dinner redeemed by the stories of the old reprobate, was immediately concerned for his welfare.

'The old bugger's fireproof in that respect. He did everything he wanted to do years ago. Now for most of the time he just reports golf for the local rag, to keep himself out of mischief, he says. Obviously without success. I was quite grateful to him for the diversion. I think the producer had set me up as a fall guy, if that's the expression.'

'You know quite well it is. Only judges are allowed to pretend they don't know phrases like that, not policemen.' His resentment of American linguistic intrusions was tolerated with affectionate resignation by those closest to him. As a teacher, Christine had a sneaking sympathy for it. 'And you underestimate your own public performances. You're well capable of creating your own diversions when you require them. Anyway, what was edited out? Are you about to unmask the killer at the Wye Castle?'

Lambert's face wrinkled with displeasure at so amateurish a conception of detection. 'We're getting nearer. I have an inkling, but I might be quite wrong.'

'Don't say you're playing a hunch. Cyril Burgess would be delighted with the idea.'

John Lambert smiled wanly. The pathologist paraded his reading of crime

223

literature, even American crime literature, at the slightest hint of encouragement. 'I'd like to be able to make an arrest before the golfing group disperses. That means a lot of work tomorrow. Bert has arranged for me to see Harrington's widow first thing in the morning. I have a feeling she may hold the key to this.'

In a way he could not foresee on that quiet evening, he was quite right.

CHAPTER TWENTY

Marie Harrington was glad to get out of her hotel. It was comfortable, but its small rooms were increasingly claustrophobic. It was a relief to escape to the vast, anonymous darkness of the night outside.

She glanced at the tiny watch on her left wrist in the last of the light from the hotel's frontage. It was five minutes after half past ten. She was deliberately a few minutes after the appointed time, for she did not want to wait alone at the rendezvous. Even in these quiet parts, a woman might be unwise to wander alone at night.

There was more wind than she had expected, but it was not cold. She glanced at the sky and remembered a line she had learned years ago at school: 'The moon was a ghostly galleon, tossed upon cloudy seas.' This night's almost full moon was not exactly tossed, but it was intermittently obscured by swiftly moving dark patches. She couldn't remember the next line of a poem she thought she had forgotten for ever: something about the road being a ribbon of moonlight, she thought. Well, that was fair enough: the lane which branched off the hotel road and ran away towards the river looked almost white in the light of the new moon, until it disappeared beneath the high trees near the river. She gathered her short summer coat about her and set off vigorously to her meeting.

Her footsteps rang loud upon the silent lane. The only natural sound was a screech-owl from the woods ahead of her, but it was quiet enough for her to catch faintly the scream of a car's brakes away towards Hereford. She was not frightened of the dark, she told herself resolutely. She had been brought up in Wiltshire countryside, where there was no such thing as street lighting, and she had not been allowed the girlish fears of the suburban adolescent. Now she reverted to her youthful reaction to disquiet at night, and walked even more briskly.

Her eyes grew more accustomed to the limited light from the full moon, as she knew they would. In five minutes, she caught the silver mirror of the river, where it curved in a wide bend beneath the trees. Half a mile away the castellations of the Wye Castle loomed for a moment against the night sky, a black, evocative silhouette that disappeared even as she watched when a patch of cloud obscured the moon.

It was around here that they had arranged to meet. She hesitated, then passed on reluctantly into the black shadow of the trees. With the moon still clouded, she could scarcely see enough to follow the road here. It was past the agreed time for the meeting; her partner in it was perhaps as nervous about being here alone as she felt herself. She called the name tentatively; it seemed to bounce back from the wall of darkness ahead of her.

Then, after she had faltered forward another few steps, a low voice from the trees on her right, between her and the now invisible river said urgently, 'Marie?'

'Who else at this hour?' she said irritably. 'Surely there was no need for all this cloak and dagger stuff?' But she was relieved to feel another human presence in that silent place, despite herself. When the shadow detached itself from the deeper blackness behind it and came softly to her side, she had to resist an impulse to reach out and touch it, to give herself the tactile reassurance of a friendly presence.

As if to confirm her safety, the moon reappeared after its brief oblivion, dappling the narrow lane with patches of silver where it filtered between the high branches of beech and oak. 'It was necessary to be cautious,' said the companion beside her. 'The police are watching all of us, and I'm afraid we're even beginning to watch each other. But I don't think my absence from the Wye Castle will be noticed at this time.'

The voice sounded as strained as her own; she wondered how much the setting was contributing to their tension. It was a long time since she had made an assignation like this at night, and then it had had other, more romantic, connotations. 'I might have enjoyed a stroll by the Wye in darkness at one time. I'm getting a little long in the tooth for it now!' she said. Her nervous giggle rang brittle as glass amid the trees.

Her companion said nothing. After a few seconds, Marie remembered her feeling of gratitude earlier in the day and her resolution to express it. 'I wanted to thank you,' she said awkwardly. 'To thank you for delivering me from Guy.' It sounded as silly as she felt, and she said no more. She wished the person who had arranged this strange meeting had more to say. They were almost beside the river itself now; she felt herself steered gently through a gateway and on to the bank. 'The farmer won't be pleased to find that left open,' she said edgily.

'I opened it, just now,' said the voice at her side. It was breathy, unnaturally harsh, and a gust of bad breath engulfed her briefly with the statement.

She felt without knowing why that this was the first clear evidence of a danger she should have acknowledged much earlier. Desperately she said, 'I don't want to know any more, you know. I just wanted to assure you that you're quite safe as far—'

Suddenly she was in the water, with hands pressing inexorably upon her shoulders. The water was no more than three or four feet deep, but she was off balance. The sudden coldness ran like a shock through her whole body. It was not until her head was beneath its surface that she realized that she was fighting for her life.

The struggle was brief and unavailing. The hands pressed steadily upon her shoulders and the back of her neck. Her feet fought unsuccessfully to get a grip on the muddy bed of the Wye. With the relentless pressure downwards which was applied, she could not even rise to her knees. She could not believe the other's hands had such strength.

As the water burst into the lungs of Marie Harrington it was not her past life which flashed in vivid retrospect before her. Her last thought was of her own stupidity in coming to such a place at such a time. And to meet such a companion.

Once her slim body had ceased its brief and violent struggle, her adversary cautiously removed the gloved hands from her back. The corpse was gently eased towards the middle of the river, where the slow current bore it away downstream. A torch flashed briefly over the river's bank, checking for any obvious traces of the brief struggle.

When the dark shadow had moved back to the road, it removed the plastic bags which had covered its feet, disguising the imprints of sole and heel.

Then, darkly silhouetted in the moonlight like the instrument of death it was, it moved swiftly and silently back towards the Wye Castle.

FRIDAY

CHAPTER TWENTY-ONE

Alison Munro moved with uncharacteristic stealth. She was not used to disguising her actions from others, but on this occasion there had been no alternative.

Her first visit to the place on the previous evening had been under the cover of darkness, and there had been little chance of detection. Now, the early-morning light seemed brilliant, even harsh, and she felt that there was no way that her actions would not be detected. But it was scarcely after six, though the sun was already so bright, and no curious eye peeped around the drawn curtains behind her.

She checked briefly, but thoroughly, on what she had come here to see. As far as her untrained eye could judge, all was satisfactory. She looked all around her, feeling a furtiveness that was quite foreign. Then, lifted by a relief she had no need to disguise, she turned and went back towards her room.

The evidence seemed effectively destroyed.

* * *

'Check Mrs Harrington's room, please.' Lambert's face was grey with foreboding.

'It's not our policy to disturb guests in the mornings, Superintendent. We could get the chambermaid to look in and—'

'Now!' It was a shout, a fierce, impersonal order. The starchy receptionist leapt into action as though she had been hit. 'I want to know whether the bed has been slept in,' he flung after her rapidly disappearing back.

The woman was back in two minutes, prickly with resentment, but cowed by the news she brought. 'Mrs Harrington isn't there. Her bed hasn't been slept in. As far as I can see, her clothes are still in the room, and she hasn't packed.' She seemed to find a bleak comfort in this last fact; perhaps she thought it indicated that the customer had not departed without payment.

'If she turns up, please ring Oldford police

230

station immediately. It's very important.' His tone was neutral, but his face told her that he thought such a reappearance most unlikely. 'Meantime, will you try to find out when she was last seen here, please?'

While she went off into the hotel kitchen, Bert Hook bustled in breathlessly from the hotel car park. 'Her car is still there. Engine cold: it certainly hasn't been used this morning.'

'Get Rushton to put out a full alert. I don't think for a moment that she'll be there, but he'd better set up a check round her home area to see if anyone has seen her. Get a description round the Hereford beat men who were operating last night to see if anyone saw her.' Hook knew the routine well enough and so did Rushton: a single terse instruction would have been enough. Lambert was talking to relieve his own tension.

The receptionist came back, her face clouded now with the concern she had caught from them. 'The night porter says he saw her go out at about half past ten, or maybe a little later. He didn't see her come back, but he isn't on duty all night. He goes off between twelve and one. Our guests have keys.'

Women vanished often enough, usually for reasons which did not warrant police attention. Without any evidence yet to hand, both of them felt already that this disappearance was sinister.

*   *   *

In the Murder Room at the Wye Castle,
detective-sergeants and constables moved on
large and careful feet, keeping an eye on the
chief who was so uncharacteristically disturbed
by the absence of a woman who had seemed to
most of them only on the periphery of the
case. Lambert was not even conscious that he
was treated warily, or that he spoke to any of
them harshly. His fury was with himself, for
not anticipating this development and
frustrating it.

He pursued his investigation now like a man
driven by some outside force. The Munros felt
it immediately, but he gave them no
explanation for the cold dynamism that cut
through the normal politeness of dialogue.

It was turned first upon Alison. 'You lied
about your movements on the night of
Harrington's death. Why?'

She was thrown on to the defensive by his
abruptness. 'I am not in the habit of lying,' she
said stiffly. 'What makes you think—'

'You were heard having a row with
Harrington when you said you were wandering
round the outside of the hotel buildings.'

'Who told you—'

'It doesn't matter who told me. Do you deny
it?'

She looked at him furiously. She had such a

232

natural, unconscious superiority in her bearing that it was a long time since anyone had spoken to her like this. Lambert was so intense that he was totally unaware of his manner. Perhaps she realized it, for she said, 'No. It's true. We had an argument. I suppose others must have heard.'

'What about?'

'Do you have to know?' Her dark eyes flashed across the grim faces opposite her; what she saw there made her fear an outburst from Lambert, so that she answered herself. 'Yes, I suppose you do. Damn Guy Harrington! He's still causing trouble after he's dead.' She glanced sideways at her husband; suddenly the proud set of her head disappeared and she was vulnerable, wondering what reaction her revelations would elicit from that taciturn presence she relied upon so much.

'It's the oldest story in the book. Guy was trying to get between the sheets with me. He had been trying for several months.'

'And did the determined Mr Harrington offer anything in the way of persuasion for you to acquiesce?' Lambert's phrasing, edged with sarcasm and suggesting his scepticism, made her eyes flash angrily. But he was careless of her feelings in what might have been a delicate area; she had lied once and might do so again.

'He was persuasive and threatening by turns. He couldn't believe I wouldn't

233

cooperate eventually. I should have sent him packing to start with.'

'So why didn't you?' Hook watched Munro clenching his fists beside his wife; perhaps it was the question he had himself been asking. He did not look at Alison. His eyes stared at Lambert as unblinkingly as if he was in a trance.

'I wasn't a free agent. Sandy works—worked—for Guy, as you know. I think you may also know that he wasn't well treated. Several of what should have been his patents had been appropriated by Harrington. "Standard business practice," he called it!' She spat the phrase with a bitterness that was almost tangible. Her husband's hand stole slowly across to cover hers, though his eyes never left Lambert's face.

Alison Munro's concentration was so fierce that she was startled by the touch; a little, involuntary shudder ran through her before she brought across her other hand to give her husband's tight fingers a brief answering squeeze. She said, 'I was foolish enough to think I could appeal to Guy's better nature. He treated it as an offer to grab what he wanted. He said that if I became his mistress he would see that Sandy was suitably rewarded for his talents.'

'And you refused.' It was a statement, not a question. She glanced up, prepared to be offended, but found the same strangely neutral

234

intensity in her inquisitor.

'I refused. That only brought out the bully that was never far beneath the surface in Guy. He turned from persuasion to threats. If he hadn't held all the cards, it would have been laughable. He was like an operatic villain.'

'Scarpia, by the sound of it.'

She nodded, showing no sign of surprise that a detective should make such a reference, staring down gratefully at the reddish hairs on the back of the neat hand that still covered hers. 'He threatened that he would sack Sandy. When I laughed in his face and said that a good engineer wouldn't be out of work for long, he invited me to test that theory. He said that if I didn't cooperate he'd make damned sure that Sandy never worked again.'

She suddenly twitched her head to look rather wildly at her husband. 'It might have been rubbish, I don't know. But he sounded very convincing. I believed him, for a time at least. I should have—'

'What exactly was the subject of your final argument with Harrington?' Lambert dragged her attention ruthlessly back from her own emotions to the facts of his investigation.

'I went back to tell him to get lost, once and for all. He tried first to cajole and then to threaten me again, and suddenly I could stand it no longer. I screamed at him, I think. Anyway, I told him to do what the hell he wanted. But if Sandy suffered, he'd better look out for himself.' It was the kind of airy, unsupported threat that policemen heard often. But coming so inappropriately from this coolly classic beauty, it sounded full of genuine menace.

'Did you threaten to kill him?'

She looked at him with a sudden fear. 'I may well have done. I certainly felt like it.' She hesitated momentarily, then said, as though defending herself was a concession, 'However, I didn't murder him.'

'Nevertheless, he was dead within half an hour of your final rejection of him.'

For the first time in their exchanges, Lambert allowed himself a pause. Even now, it was a brief one, and he made no reference to the notes in front of him. Nor did his eyes leave the woman's face as he said, 'Mr Munro, can you show me the sweater you were wearing on the day of the murder? It was a blue one, I think, with strands of white wool woven into the pattern.'

Sandy Munro looked shaken for a moment: whether by the request itself, the precision of Lambert's description, or the suddenness of the transition from his wife's last words with Harrington, it was impossible to say. Then he said, 'Yes, I know the one. I wore it to play golf in the afternoon, as you say.' He stood up, moving for once as jerkily as a puppet. 'It should be in the wardrobe in our room, though I can't think why—'

236

'Don't bother, Sandy. It isn't there.' His wife's voice was like ice in the warm room. She spoke like one in a trance, her eyes staring straight ahead at the innocent sky outside. Then, with an effort that was obvious to them all, she wrenched her attention back to Lambert. 'Why do you want it?'

'I think you know that, Mrs Munro. Where is it?'

Her brain seemed to work with extra speed in this crisis, like a driver's in the course of a road accident. It told her that there was no point in concealment, after all. 'It doesn't exist any more. It went to the gardeners' bonfire last night. I checked that it had gone completely at six o'clock this morning.' Her eyes blazed with a desperate defiance.

'And why did you do that?' Lambert's voice registered neither surprise nor emotion.

'Because I thought you might come looking for it.'

'You were correct in that. Mrs Munro, destroying evidence can be a very serious matter. Courts have been known to take it as an admission of guilt.'

Sandy Munro had sat down again, heavily, like a boxer dumped on the canvas by a stunning blow. Alison stretched out her hand and linked her fingers through his unresisting ones. Her face was very white within its neat helmet of black hair, but she said nothing.

It was Lambert who eventually broke a

silence which seemed to have stretched far beyond the few seconds which was the reality. 'Mrs Munro, I do not have time to probe delicately after the truth. We are investigating a murder; for all we know, two murders.' He saw both their faces fix in horror upon his, but he did not even check. 'I will tell you frankly that I do not think that your husband killed Guy Harrington. I do believe, however, that he moved the body, which could certainly make him an accessory after the fact. I think that you also believe that. Perhaps, indeed, you *know* that.'

Alison Munro looked wildly from her husband to the two detectives, her senses for once in her life reeling in disarray. It was Bert Hook who prompted quietly, 'The forensic boys will probably be able to get all they want from the remains of that bonfire, Mrs Munro. I'm sure carbon analysis techniques will be able to identify a particular type of wool, even among the ashes. That's all they need, you see: they already have the sweater fibres found on the corpse.'

Perhaps his low-key, reassuring tones were what was needed. But it was not Alison but Sandy Munro who looked at him almost gratefully and said, 'All right, yes. I moved Harrington's body.'

He stopped then: perhaps in his naïvety he thought the simple acknowledgement would be enough. Lambert said, 'You lied to us also,

Mr Munro. Quite comprehensively.' Hook wondered for a moment if he was about to charge one of them with murder. Instead Lambert said only, 'You had better give us a proper account of your movements on the night of the murder now.'

Munro took a deep breath, like a child about to embark upon a full confession of some shameful escapade. 'After the party broke up, I went for a walk, as I told you.'

'Exactly as you told us?'

'Yes. I walked on my own down to the main gates of the complex. It's about three-quarters of a mile. I remember I went and stood on the green nearest to the gates in the moonlight for a moment or two.'

'You told us that your wife was already in bed and almost asleep when you got back to your room. That wasn't true, was it?'

Munro shook his head miserably, looking again like a child who has been found out. For a normally straightforward man, confessions of dishonesty, or worse, did not come easily. 'No. She wasna there at all.' Under stress, his Fifeshire accent thickened a little.

'Did that seem significant to you?'

'Not at the time. It did later.'

'You'd heard her rowing with Harrington, hadn't you?'

Munro suddenly shook his head roughly, as if trying to clear it of confusions. 'I didna know it was her, not then. But I had heard angry voices, yes. A man's and a woman's.'

'Yet you didn't think Alison was involved?'

'Not at the time I didn't. I thought it was Harrington and Meg Peters. When Alison wasn't in the room, I didn't know what to think. When she came in and went to bed without a word to me, I got to thinking it could have been her.'

'So you got up again,' prompted Hook gently. He wondered if they were on the way to a full confession, found himself hoping unprofessionally that they were not.

'Yes. I couldn't sleep. I spoke to Alison, but she seemed to be asleep. I think now that she was only pretending.' They glanced at each other; she gave him a tiny, acknowledging smile. 'I got up and put some clothes on to go for a walk round.'

'At what time?' Hook's ballpoint was poised like a recording angel's over his notebook.

'I couldn't be sure. Perhaps an hour after I'd gone to bed. Half past one, say, or a little after.' He spoke like one who anticipated that precision here might be important. Perhaps he saw himself giving this evidence in court in due course.

It was Lambert who said, 'And you found Harrington's body?'

'Yes. On the gravel path below the roof where we'd been sitting earlier.' His voice was low enough for them to have to strain after it in the quiet room.

240

'And you chose to move it. You had better tell us why.'

'I'd decided by that time that it was Alison I'd heard with Guy. When I found his body, I suppose I assumed for a moment that she'd pushed him off the roof.'

'A theory which has yet to be disproved,' said Lambert drily. 'What did you hope to achieve by moving the corpse?'

Munro looked at his wife; she gave his hand a brief, encouraging squeeze, but neither of them smiled as he went on. 'My brain wasn't working very clearly. I think I felt that others beside myself must have heard the row between Alison and Guy. As you say they did. I thought that if I moved the body out on to the course and it wasn't found until the next day, almost anyone might have done it.'

'So you hauled him into the wheelbarrow and trundled him down the fairway. And left traces of your clothing fibres on both the wheelbarrow and the corpse's clothes. Not very clever.'

'If I were more used to murder, maybe I'd think of these things!' In the relief at having his confession out, Munro showed a flash of his normal spirit.

Lambert turned his attention back to Alison. 'Did you kill Harrington?'

'No.' She looked as if at that moment she would have liked to kill Lambert.

'Can you give us any proof that you did

not?'

'No. I thought the idea of English law was that one was innocent until—'

'Have you any idea who did kill him?'

'No.'

He looked at them coldly for a moment. 'Both of you lied quite deliberately to us about your movements at the time of Harrington's death. I advise you therefore to be very careful as to your answer to this question. Where were you between ten-thirty and midnight last night?'

They looked at each other; shock and fear were in their faces. Whether it was the consternation of the innocent drawn into evil they could not comprehend or the guilty appalled that their malice had been pinpointed, it was impossible to say. Alison said, 'May we ask why you wish to know?'

Lambert shook his head even as she spoke. 'Not at present. Well?'

She answered without looking at her husband. 'We went out into Hereford at about nine. We both felt a need to get away from here. To be among people we did not know and would never see again. We had a drink in a pub. I can't remember the name; it was near the big bridge over the river.'

Hook wrote it down carefully. It could be checked, with a little leg-work by the team. Most customers would remember Alison Munro. He said, 'What time did you leave

242

there?'

She looked at her husband. Sandy Munro said, 'Before last orders. About half past ten, I suppose.'

Lambert said, 'And where did you go from there?'

Munro looked at him as if he suspected a trick question. 'Straight back here. We must have been in our room within fifteen minutes, at most.'

'Did anyone see you come in to the Wye Castle?'

'No. We parked and went straight up to our room.'

'And you didn't go out again?'

'No.'

'Or see anyone else go?'

'No. Superintendent, I think we have a right to know—'

'I'm sorry, but you must take my word that this is no time to talk of rights. Please be good enough to tell Mr Nash that I'll see him now. He's waiting outside, I hope.'

They left with dignity, despite his brusque dismissal. Hook recorded their last words carefully in his notebook. He thought them a highly devoted couple, capable of that intimacy which shuts out the rest of the world, or moulds it to their own purposes.

The squalid history of homicide showed that such couples had often planned and executed murder.

CHAPTER TWENTY-TWO

Waiting had not improved the day for Tony Nash.

He came in looking thoroughly anxious, despite his impeccable casual dress. His green sweater might have been enjoying its first outing; his darker green golf trousers were sharply creased. Lambert, who thought of golf attire as a means of using up clothes that were past their best, caught himself registering automatic disapproval of this tailor's dummy. But Nash's was an innocent enough vanity, if vanity indeed it was: a man did not have to be a murderer to indulge it.

But the immaculate clothing was an inadequate disguise for the discomfort within it. Nash could not keep still. He threw one ankle immediately across his knee, in a caricature of relaxation, but his powerful arms and torso twitched in a series of small, uncontrolled movements. It was interesting to see the way tension took men. Sandy Munro had been frozen into immobility by it, his movements when he had to make them as jerky as a puppet's. Tony Nash suffered almost an opposite reaction: striving to keep still, he could not control those small, involuntary physical movements which his too-active brain inflicted upon his body.

Lambert was as brisk as he had been with the Munros. Ruffling the sheets of Nash's original statement, he said, 'You said when we spoke to you two days ago that you thought you were the last person known to have been with Harrington when he was alive. Do you stick by that?'

Nash shifted on his chair as if it was too hot for him to remain in one position. 'No. I—I heard someone else with him after I had left.'

'So you lied to us. Will you now tell us why, please.'

Lambert's voice was quiet; ominously so, it must have seemed to Nash, who did not know that he was not the only one who had withheld the full truth. 'I thought at the time it might have been Meg, you see.' He seemed to think this explained his omission completely.

'You had better tell us what you heard. And when.'

Just voices. A man's and a woman's. Having a hell of a bust-up. The man's voice was Harrington's. I thought at the time that the woman's might have been Meg's. I know now that it must have been Alison Munro's.'

'So you choose to tell us what you heard. No doubt if it didn't suit you, you would still be withholding the information. Where were you when you heard this exchange?'

'In the car park. I told you, I went out to make sure my car boot was—'

'And what has now convinced you that the

245

woman involved was Mrs Munro?'

'I talked to Meg. Once it wasn't her, it had to be Alison: she was the only other woman around.' He ran his hand violently through his mane of yellow hair; he had thought that once he had confessed his original omission, things would have been simple enough for him.

Lambert looked at him hard for a long, speculative moment. Nash thought he was searching for further concealments, but in fact Lambert was wondering exactly how far the personable Meg Peters had taken her trusting fiancé into her confidence. How much did he know of her past and the untidy tangle of her relationship with Harrington? Eventually Lambert said, 'You told us that Mr Harrington was not a good employer. That he was exploiting you.'

Nash nodded, white-faced. He had folded his arms now, in an attempt at physical control of his too-mobile upper body, but his fingers ran like a flute-player's up and down his upper arms; Lambert remembered the mannerism from their earlier interview. 'Have you any reason to think that other employees were treated harshly?'

Nash found the question, with its temporary transfer of attention away from his own concerns, something of a relief. 'Yes, I'm sure they were. I don't know how, but I'm certain Sandy Munro was being exploited by Guy as much as I was. Sandy never says much, so I

246

couldn't give you any detail.'

'I believe George Goodman's daughter worked for the firm for a time. Do you know of any reason she had to resent Harrington?'

'Any reason why George should have killed Guy, you mean.' Nash allowed himself a small, humourless smile at the speed with which he had picked up the line of reasoning. And indeed, it would be easy to underestimate his quick brain just because he seemed insensitive in some areas, thought Lambert.

Nash said, 'She was too remote from me for me to know anything like that. She was a junior in another department: I didn't even know she was working for the firm until George told me on the golf course. Next thing I knew, she'd left. Not much for you there, I shouldn't think. But I'm sure there were other senior staff as well as me with grievances, though I haven't the detail. It's not the sort of thing one broadcasts to one's juniors.'

Nash seemed to feel the need to assert his senior position in the firm, even in this crisis. Lambert said brutally, 'And yet of recent months you have made no secret of your hatred for the owner of the firm, even before these juniors. Your fellow-workers report an extremity in your language, and a carelessness about concealment, that almost suggest paranoia.'

Nash's powerful torso shot forward and he came almost out of his seat. But his preliminary 'Now look—' dissolved as he realized to whom he was talking.

Lambert said quickly, 'Why did you cease to control a resentment which you had previously kept private? Had your employment situation changed?'

Nash looked now like a man who had been hit. His face was flushed with the strain of a series of emotions. Another one took over as he said, 'No . . . I suppose it was because of Meg. I'm going to marry her, Superintendent.'

Like all lovers, he thought the simple statement carried a wealth of greater meanings. When the two large men opposite him failed to react as he expected, he said, 'When I thought of the way Harrington had treated her, was still treating her, I sometimes couldn't stand it. Meg said to forget it, but I could see sometimes how he was getting to her, and I wasn't going to have it.'

It was the quixotic, unfocused rage of the lover who sees no outlet for his temper but is determined to vent it. It was easy to see the potential for murder in him when he allowed his imagination to dwell on images of Harrington with his wife-to-be. Lambert wondered how much Nash knew about Meg Peters's past. Did he know of her appearances in blue films? Perhaps more significantly, did Harrington?

He decided it would be kinder to take that up with Miss Peters herself. There would be

248

enough damage left among relationships after a murder investigation of this sort, without the police trampling on sensibilities more heavily than was necessary. Instead, he flashed at Nash unexpectedly, 'Why were you so ruffled on the morning after the murder of Guy Harrington?'

'Ruffled?' He tried to play for time, to collect his resources. His too-revealing face whitened for a moment with anger, as he worked out that their source for this information must be George Goodman.

Lambert said impatiently, 'It's a straightforward enough idea, surely. Are you denying that you seemed rather preoccupied, even before the discovery of the corpse?'

'No. I suppose I was.'

'Why?' Lambert gave the impression that his patience was almost exhausted.

'I—hadn't slept much.' Perhaps it sounded lame, even in his own ears, for Nash went on quickly, 'Meg and I talked a long way into the night about what Guy had done to her. And—'

'Did you leave your room again during the night?'

He looked from one face to the other, finding no clue in either to what they knew. He must have decided they knew more than they did, for he said with an air of hopelessness, 'All right, yes, I did. I don't know who told you. I found Guy's body on the gravel path beneath the roof where we had—'

'When?' Lambert used the monosyllable like a weapon.

'I—I'm not sure. Perhaps forty minutes, fifty minutes after Meg and I had got back to our room. After what we'd been discussing, I felt the need for some fresh—'

'He was quite dead then. You're sure?'

Nash nodded; his face had gone white now with the recollection. 'I didn't take his pulse, but I held my watch near his mouth. It didn't mist up and I knew—'

'How was he lying?'

'Face down. Not the way he was when we found him on the golf course.'

'You felt no call to do your duty and report his death?'

Nash shook his head stubbornly, looking at the carpet between them as though it held some mystic code. 'No. I was glad he was dead. At that moment, that was all I could feel.'

'Did you tell anyone of your discovery?'

'No. I might have told Meg, but she was asleep by that time. I sat in the bedroom armchair for a long time.'

It was a strange picture: this strongly built man sitting in the darkness, hugging to himself his exultation in the death of his powerful enemy, senses reeling as he wondered who might have rid him of this scourge.

'And you went out again soon after six next morning.'

'Yes. I think I dozed for an hour or so, but I

couldn't sleep. I think I was hoping that someone would have discovered the body to save me reporting it, but I ran into George Goodman instead. He'd seen me through his window.'

'Yes. And did he, like you, appear distraught?'

Nash swallowed hard and took time to think: this time they could not object to that. It was an opportunity to inculpate the urbane architect, and all three of them were conscious of that. Eventually Nash shook his head. 'No, I don't think so. He said he hadn't slept well, but he looked to me as trim as he usually does.'

'And what about when you eventually found the body on the course? Did Goodman seem surprised to find it there?'

Nash paused again. It was as if he saw the opportunity to lift suspicion from himself by incriminating Goodman, but his sense of fair play would not allow him to do so. 'I really couldn't say, Superintendent. George was shocked enough, I'm sure. He more or less took charge of things immediately—it was he who informed the police—but that was quite in character. I was too stunned myself to register anything very clearly. I'd been nerving myself to the discovery of the body while we were on the course, you see, thinking that surely one of the hotel staff must have found it by that time. Finding it in that hollow beside the twelfth was a real shock to me. I couldn't work it out at all. Still can't, for that matter.'

Lambert said formally, as though reciting a legal formula, 'Mr Nash, you have admitted withholding vital information earlier in this investigation. You have made no secret of the fact that you were glad to see Harrington lying dead; indeed, you said during our previous meeting that your first instinct was to protect his killer. I therefore ask you now whether you have any idea who killed Guy Harrington.'

Nash paused just long enough, allowed the right troubled expression to steal across his face. If he was dissimulating, he did it well. 'No, I haven't. We've tried to discuss it among the group, you know. But the knowledge that one of us is probably responsible tends to get in the way.' He gave them an ironic smile, and indeed the idea of a killer sitting down with innocent companions to a serious review of the facts surrounding a murder had a decided touch of black comedy. 'Tell me, Superintendent, do you know who moved the body?'

Lambert smiled and Hook, intervening nervously as if he feared his chief's eccentric habits, said stiffly, 'If we did, Mr Nash, we wouldn't be able to discuss it with you.'

Lambert said abruptly, 'Have you spoken to Mrs Harrington since the death of her husband?'

Nash looked surprised. 'No. I saw her here on the day of the murder, and George

Goodman told me that she's still around, but—'

'Would you tell us where you were between ten-thirty and midnight last night, please?'

Nash was shaken. He wondered if Marie Harrington had said anything about him to Goodman when she had talked to him. 'I—I was here, I think. Yes, that's right.'

Hook said quietly, 'Are there witnesses to that, Mr Nash?' The blank sheet of his notebook shone like an admonition towards rectitude as he paused with pen above it.

'Only Meg. We—we were in bed by that time. It's our last night here and we had been pretty disturbed previously by—'

'You had retired, then, by half past ten?' Hook was studiously impassive, having learned long since not to allow speculation about the bedroom activities of members of the public to show in his face or voice. 'No doubt Miss Peters will confirm this for us in due course.'

Nash nodded, trying to appear as imperturbable as his questioners. But when dismissed, he left the room eagerly, even more nervous than when he had entered it.

Lambert made no attempt to prevent him from contacting his fiancée. He had no doubt that she would support Nash's story where necessary.

CHAPTER TWENTY-THREE

Marie Harrington's body was found at noon.

An elderly fisherman, near the centre of Hereford, was dozing in the midday sun, enjoying the peace of the river and the absence of his wife's nagging. The body drifted close to the bank without his noticing it. Undulating lightly with the gentle downstream motion, it nosed gently but insistently against his net at the edge of the water, like an old dog demanding attention.

The man was a pillar of the British Legion; he had seen death in plenty as a young man in the Western Desert. But that was half a century ago, and the wide, unseeing eyes and blood-tinged froth around the mouth of this corpse upset him. He was old-fashioned enough to be distressed more because it was a woman. He was greatly relieved when the police deposited him back with the wife he had been so anxious to escape two hours earlier.

*   *   *

Lambert was preparing to meet Meg Peters when DI Rushton brought him the news. 'A drowning, pretty certainly, they say. Suicide, do you think, sir?'

'Murder, Chris. I'd stake my career, or

what's left of it, on that.'

'We'll have to wait for the post-mortem to be sure. No obvious marks of violence on the body, but no doubt Dr Burgess will be able to tell us more in due course. It's not so uncommon, of course, for a survivor to follow a deceased spouse out of the world while still depressed.' Rushton had an unfortunate habit of appearing to instruct experienced officers.

'Not this spouse. I've never seen a widow facing the rest of her life more eagerly than the bereaved Mrs Harrington.'

'You think the two deaths are connected, then?'

'I'm sure they are. I was due to see her first thing this morning. I think she knew more than she had told us previously—possibly even the identity of her husband's killer. Certainly that killer thought she must be removed before she could reveal anything to me.'

'What about the hotel where she was staying? Do they know who contacted her?'

'No. Not so far, anyway. She seems to have gone out at about ten thirty-five last night. In all probability, she never returned. Damn the Chief Constable and his press conferences! I'd have seen her yesterday, if I hadn't had to hare off to Gloucester.' He slammed the door of the filing cabinet violently shut. At that moment, he had no room for compassion for the dead woman. The policeman in him had taken over, and he had room only for the

255

frustration stemming from the removal of a vital witness from the case.

*   *   *

It took Bert Hook, who came into the room as Rushton went out, to restore the human dimension to this death. 'I feel as though I let her down,' he said dully. 'If I'd pressed harder yesterday . . . She seemed a nice woman.' The very lameness of this made it a touching tribute.

'Oh, shut up, Bert!' The Sergeant's troubled face was like a rebuke to his callousness. Lambert would have his regrets for the woman—later, when there was time. At the moment, she was a woman who might have cleared up the mystery of her husband's death by now, but had chosen to withhold the information, and paid for it with her life. 'Didn't she tell you anything, yesterday afternoon. Think, for God's sake.'

Hook shook his head miserably. 'Nothing that seemed significant. I've told you most of it already. She stonewalled. She didn't know why Tony Nash was so open in his hatred of her husband. She thought Sandy Munro was "a poppet" with a nice wife. She didn't even know that George Goodman's daughter had worked for her husband, and couldn't see any reason for him to want her husband out of the way. She obviously hadn't much time for Meg

Peters, but she assured me that she didn't think she was connected with the death.'

'In other words, Bert, she went out of her way to assure you of everyone's innocence. With an even-handedness which argues that she knew which one of them had murdered the husband she was glad to see removed, but wasn't inclined to reveal it. Didn't she seem defensive about any particular one, for God's sake?'

'No. I could have pressed harder, but I'd only gone to make arrangements for you to see her this morning. I wouldn't have seen her at all if she'd been answering the phone.'

'No, I know, Bert. It's as well you got as much as you did out of her. If we can find the area where she was concealing something, we may be there. Did you check anything else with her.'

'Only her own whereabouts on the night of her husband's death. She was with another man at the vital time, she says, back in Surrey. It should be easy enough to check. Perhaps we'd better.' Hook knew well enough that the lover who worked with the wife to remove an unwanted husband was a common enough combination in homicide.

'In due course, if we have to. But I think our solution is somewhere here.'

'Here at present, John.' Hook's rare use of the chief's forename marked the resumption of their normal easy working relationship. 'But not for much longer. The group is due to break up and go home this afternoon.'

With events teeming fast upon each other, Lambert had all but forgotten what he had himself arranged three days earlier. In five hours the Wye Castle party would disperse. 'We can't hold them any longer, I'm afraid. Not even another night. I'm surprised we haven't had lawyers brandished at us before now by someone. I suppose they all thought it might be construed as an admission of guilt.'

'And it's not too unpleasant a place to be detained,' said Hook, gazing through the picture window of the murder room at the azure sky and the green world beneath it. It was the nearest he would come to acknowledging the attractions of golf; he was looking loftily over the course to the panorama of woods and river beyond it. Far away towards the skyline, a tractor, too distant to be heard, crawled slowly uphill, a reminder of the normal world which seemed at the moment so far removed from them.

'Wheel in the dangerous Miss Peters,' said his superintendent. His frustration and ill-temper were removed by the prospect of work and the peculiar concentration it demanded.

Meg Peters was a diverting enough figure in her own right. Her dark brown trews displayed her lower limbs to admirable effect. The russet blouse might have clashed with her lustrous dark red hair, but instead appeared to complement it perfectly. The slim gold chain deposited its gold cross naturally between the curves of her breasts, as if drawing discreet attention to what was decently hidden beneath the silk. If her husband-to-be had been conspicuously nervous, she exuded confidence.

It might, of course, be a carefully contrived mime: she was, after all, an actress. Lambert addressed himself to that. 'At our last meeting, we mentioned your criminal record.'

The green eyes flashed her anger, but she kept perfect control. 'Surely we can let that old business die. Or do you like to hound people for—'

'No.' It was as curt as a command to a straying animal, and it stopped her in her tracks just as effectively. 'We don't hound people, Miss Peters. But our task is made more difficult when people withhold information from us. It makes us suspicious— as it is our duty to be in cases of serious crime. And when we dig and find something which has been concealed, it naturally makes us wonder what else has been hidden from us.'

'And what else do you claim to have found?' She managed to give an edge of contempt to her question, as though she were in control of this. To that end, she kept her body apparently relaxed. But the upright position she adopted was not a natural one for her. She was no more than five feet from him, so that he could see the whitening of her knuckles as her fingers grasped the wooden arms of her chair.

'We found that you had appeared in some highly questionable scenes in at least one blue film. And became as a result a prosecution witness in a court case.'

Now she was really shaken. For a moment the green eyes darkened and narrowed with hatred. She said nothing for a moment, getting control of her breathing as though it were a professional challenge to her to speak evenly. 'What use do you propose to make of this information?'

'None whatsoever. If you can convince us that it has nothing to do with these deaths.'

'Deaths?' If she had prior knowledge of the second one, she was not falling into the easy trap.

'Mrs Harrington was found dead about half an hour ago.'

She gasped now, abandoning any effort at control of her shock. Or simulating an assumed surprise that she had practised in front of her mirror. 'Murdered?'

'I think so, Miss Peters. It's interesting you should assume so as well.'

'Marie wasn't the type for suicide.'

'Indeed.' He didn't pursue what that type might be. He had seen some unlikely suicides in the last twenty years, but he had no intention of discussing them with Meg Peters. 'Did Guy Harrington know about your appearances in these dubious films?'

She said wearily, 'They were a long time ago now. I was a young actress. In the business, you take anything to get work, when you start. Equity cards and all that. I was naïve enough then to believe the promises that blue movies would lead to other work. They didn't, of course.'

Suddenly the hoarse croak of a magpie came unnaturally loud through the open window on her right; she twisted her head to the sound, and kept it there, as if scorning to see what Lambert's reaction to her words might be. Her nose was perhaps a fraction too strong, but it was a dramatic and impressive profile against the light. Ironically in view of their present conversation, Lambert could see her as Shaw's Saint Joan, chasing cowardly soldiers and pusillanimous monarchs before her.

He said, 'I'm not interested in the morality of pornographic films. That's been dealt with long ago, in other places, thank God. What I asked you is whether Harrington knew about them.'

She sighed. 'He did. I don't know how he found out. I gave up wondering about things like that a long time ago. Guy made it his business to find out things people didn't want him to know.'

'You didn't tell him at the time when you were his mistress?'

She turned back full face to him with her

261

eyes flashing anger from the pale features. 'No. Surprising as it may seem to you, I wasn't proud of that part of my life. I thought I'd put it behind me for ever. It's taken the police to drag it out again.' There was a curious combination of bitterness and resignation in her words; he wondered what unfortunate experiences she had had in the past with police coarseness; there were many officers who would glory in the reduction of a strikingly beautiful woman to the level of the prostitutes they arrested each week.

'I gave you the chance to tell us yourself, Miss Peters, but you chose to attempt to hide it.' She acknowledged the point with a curt nod. 'Does Tony Nash know about the films?'

Though she should have expected it, the suddenness of the question caught her off guard. Her cheeks flared as if her face had been slapped, and she was suddenly more vulnerable than they had ever seen her. 'No. I suppose you're going to tell him . . . Do you people ever consider the harm you do?'

'Very often, despite what you may think. But we are charged with investigating a brutal murder. That takes priority over everything else. Now: Harrington knew. How did he propose to use the information?' Both of them presumed that the murder victim had used the knowledge unscrupulously and for his own ends. The investigation had taught the CID a lot about him, at any rate. The first rule in any inquiry was to find out as much as possible about the victim and his habits.

'He used it to taunt me. No, more than that, to threaten me. At first he just enjoyed the power it gave him. Then, when he had discarded me, he used it to humiliate me. When he took up with Felicity Goodman, he liked to set her innocence against my record as a scarlet woman, or worse.'

'Harrington had an affair with Goodman's daughter?' Hook made the question as low-key as he could, not even looking up from his notebook.

'Briefly, yes. The poor girl had no idea what he was about, I'm sure. I scarcely knew her: I thought at the time he had seduced her merely to upset me with a virgin. She had some kind of breakdown I think. Marie Harrington could tell you about it—'

She stopped, her right hand thrust to her mouth in her first unconsidered movement since she had entered the room. Suddenly she was weeping, silently, without the retching sobs shock usually brought with it. 'I'd forgotten she was dead . . . I think Marie felt a crazy kind of guilt for her husband. I know she visited the girl in hospital.'

Lambert brought her back gently but insistently to his query. 'Did Harrington threaten to tell Tony Nash about the blue films?'

She was broken now, anxious only to explain

herself, not resist them. 'Yes. He taunted me with the threat. That was how he insulted me on the night of his death, when Tony took up the cudgels for me.' There was a brief flash of pride in the last phrase, and they realized that the affection between this striking, experienced woman and the vain, rather shallow man she had chosen probably ran deeper than anything either of the parties had ever experienced before. 'I don't expect you to understand this, Superintendent, but Tony is rather old-fashioned in some respects. He will be shocked by the news of those films. I shall tell him in my own time, but I want to choose that time myself.'

Lambert privately thought that after the first shock, Nash was the sort of man who would be excited rather than repelled by the knowledge, but he kept his own counsel. This job was difficult enough without taking on its social worker aspects. He dismissed her rather abruptly, anxious to make use of her revelations in the limited time available before the group broke up and returned home.

She stood up awkwardly, surprised that her ordeal had been terminated so swiftly. Fumbling in her bag for a handkerchief, she said, 'I suppose the thought that Guy might have revealed this to Tony gave me an added motive to kill him.' It was unexpectedly conciliatory, almost as though she wished in the end to prolong the interview. Perhaps she wanted to repair some of the damage to her eye make-up before she rejoined her lover; she dabbed vigorously at her tears with a handkerchief too delicate for the task.

Lambert was almost drawn into the brutal rejoinder that if Nash knew—he half-suspected Harrington had told him after all in their final exchange after the party had broken up on the fatal night—it gave him too an added motive for murder. The violent thrusting of a man into the darkness from that roof was just the sort of crime to be produced by a red mist of fury following such a taunt.

Instead, the Superintendent held his peace, dismissing her with one of the standard injunctions of his trade about not revealing to others what she had told him. Then he went back to the filing cabinet he had slammed so vigorously when he heard the news of Marie Harrington's drowning half an hour earlier.

Amid the masses of data which accrued in the days following a murder, there was usually some vital detail which needed to be pinpointed. It had taken a second, totally unnecessary death to identify this one.

He took out a file and extracted the phone numbers he needed.

CHAPTER TWENTY-FOUR

It was almost four o'clock. The group who had come to the Wye Castle so full of noisy hilarity were preparing to leave it in subdued mood.

All of them except one, that is. Even three days after his death, the baleful presence of Guy Harrington was still strong among them as they prepared to leave the scene of his murder. Inside the residential block, the door of his room remained securely locked, a blank reminder as they passed of the retribution his murder would bring for one of them. Outside it, Harrington's black Jaguar with its double headlights surveyed them unblinkingly from the other end of the car park as they prepared to go. From deep within the murder room, John Lambert and Bert Hook, their frenzied series of phone calls at last completed, watched with interest.

The Munros studiously avoided contemplation of the car as they loaded their bags systematically into their Vauxhall Carlton. Sandy hurried indoors as soon as the boot lid was down, but Alison took a defiant, unhurried look around her before she disappeared. She cast her dark eyes upwards at the new-leaved splendour of the mighty oaks and the burgeoning candelabra of the chestnut flowers, as if by doing so she could lift herself

266

above the sordid events of the last few days.

Meg Peters loaded a series of smallish bags into the back seat of Tony Nash's car. Then Nash brought out their expensive suitcases and stowed them carefully around his golf clubs and trolley in the boot. He looked apprehensively towards the murder room, but the CID men were too far within the room to be visible from outside. Meg Peters brought her last package, a dress still in its carrier from the Hereford store, and placed it reverently among the rest of her packing within the car.

For a moment the two of them stood close together in silent contemplation of the murder victim's car, as if ridding themselves in that moment of the final hold the dead man held over them. Then, like two young lovers finding each other for the first time, they linked hands and moved back into the apartment block without a backward glance. A men's four-ball on the way to the first tee, unconscious of police observation, gestured their envy of Tony Nash in unmistakable fashion, then went in search of the lesser delights of golf.

George Goodman was more leisured about his preparations for departure than any of the others. He had but a single large bag to stow in the capacious Rover. Having deposited it, he sauntered for a moment around the car park, making no attempt to avoid the black Jaguar in its isolated position at the top. Indeed, he strolled up to the car and walked along the side of it, a benevolent smile suffusing his features as he took his farewell of the man none of them had loved and most of them had hated.

Then he picked his way through the first creamy fallings of chestnut blossom to take a last look at the golf course and the river below, winding blue and slow beneath the sun towards the spot where Marie Harrington had met her death. His bearing was so dignified, his manner so august, that Hook half-expected him to confer an episcopal blessing upon the scene before he left it. Instead, he turned and walked with the same measured tread back towards his room; the benign smile he had worn throughout was still upon his lips as he disappeared.

The manager of the Wye Castle could scarcely disguise his relief at the return to normality which the departure of these guests would confirm. After the day of the murder and the removal of the body, the course had been open to those golfers who came simply to play, and they had come in their normal numbers, pausing only to register the police presence in the apartment blocks before they tackled the problems of the course.

But residents had been forbidden, apart from the five who were being so intensively investigated by the police. The hotel group's regional director had been most reluctant to adjust the manager's sales targets to take account of this. Now the restrictions had been lifted; from tomorrow, the Wye Castle Hotel and Country Club would be back to normal. Bookings might even increase, with the dubious glamour conferred on the place by a brutal murder; after the recent publicity, the manager was hopeful that considerable numbers of the kind of people who slowed their cars to look at road accidents might book in with him.

Perhaps because he felt guilty that he should be so delighted to see them go, he had laid on a farewell afternoon tea for the five who had been his only guests for the last three days. The service was attentive, for the staff were delighted to be working again after their enforced inactivity. The cakes and scones were freshly baked, the jam made on the premises, the china delicately patterned. The room, with patio doors opening on to a terrace overlooking the bowling green, the eighteenth hole and the river, was as pleasant as any in the whole of the Wye Castle's extensive range.

Yet the conversation was stilted, with long pauses between sporadic sentences. If the manager who danced such dutiful attendance was in reality anxious to see them gone, the five gave the impression that only the uncertain glue of politeness held them together. They too were anxious to be away from this pleasantest of spots as soon as decency would allow. They had had enough of

269

public exchanges, and were eager now for the cocoons of comfort and privacy afforded to them by their cars.

This awkward gathering received the entry of Lambert and Hook almost as a relief. To the five people trying so unsuccessfully to enjoy themselves, the policemen seemed at first to bring an end of term air to the gathering, like masters who had been sternly unbending while conducting classes, but were now relaxing as their charges prepared to depart. Hook saw no reason to disillusion the little gathering too quickly, especially when George Goodman hastened forward with a plate of thickly buttered scones.

'Do share in our final little indulgence together, gentlemen,' he said. The Sergeant took a scone and put it carefully on the small plate Meg Peters pushed towards him.

It was Lambert, refusing tea and cake absently, almost rudely, who changed the atmosphere from nervous hilarity to something much more tense. 'Why didn't you tell me about your daughter?' he said abruptly.

For an instant, it was not even clear whom he was addressing. Then George Goodman put down the cakes with a clatter that rang loud in the suddenly silent room. He said with a last attempt to retain his genial exterior, 'If you mean me, Superintendent, I—'

'Of course I mean you.' Lambert's voice was harsh. It was the second murder, the one he

270

felt he might have prevented, which sprang before him now, thrusting away the sympathy he might otherwise have felt for the man. 'Did you really think you could keep your daughter permanently hidden?'

Goodman sat down awkwardly, like one fearing a faint but not quite sure of where the chair was behind him. 'I don't want her brought into this,' he said dully.

Lambert said more gently, 'Harrington seduced her, didn't he?' The old-fashioned word seemed justified in this case.

There was a moment when the silence in the room seemed a tangible thing, likely to harm any of them who broke it. Except the central figure, sitting on the edge of his armchair with head bent and the white fringe of tonsorial hair more than ever apparent. Eventually he said, without facing his questioner, 'Yes. He had her, then laughed about it.'

He looked up then, and his drained and haggard face shocked his friends so much that two of them shrank involuntarily back in their seats. 'Felicity is what the doctors call "retarded", Superintendent. Nothing visible, you understand, but "not suitable for normal schooling". She is "dependent on a loving home environment".' His bitterness against what life had dealt him made him put the series of phrases into inverted commas, as an emphasis on the grim reality that lay behind the anodyne words.

'I thought Harrington was doing me a favour when he provided her with part-time work in his office. Perhaps he was, at first. He liked everyone to be under some kind of obligation to him; maybe there was nothing worse than that in the gesture.'

He stopped for so long that even Lambert, always patient in the course of a confession, had to prompt him with, 'But it didn't stop there?'

'No. She didn't do much more than make tea and coffee and run little errands around the works. Harrington's secretary was teaching her to file, and she liked that. But I don't suppose she'd ever have been able to do it on her own.' There was something horrible about the way he spoke of the girl continually in the past tense. 'She seemed to know that Guy had given her a chance she had to take. Anyway, she liked him. And one night when she was the only one left in his office . . .' He thrust his face into his hands; a moment later, they heard him weeping.

Lambert said, 'Where is your daughter now, Mr Goodman?'

'In a mental home. A "hospital for the treatment of psychiatric disorders".' Again he put the euphemism between bitter quotation marks. 'There was an abortion, you see. The bastard couldn't even take care of that!' His voice rose to a shout on the thought, and it seemed he might not be able to go any further.

But his tone became calm, even tender, as he returned to the tortured girl. 'She comes home occasionally, but she has to go back. She wouldn't harm a kitten, but they can't get her stable, you see.' They felt his wretchedness and distress, and the greater evil they now knew was to come.

'Did you plan to kill Harrington this week?' For a moment, Lambert's tone was that of the nurse.

Goodman looked at him now, seeming to register the surroundings which had disappeared from him as he re-lived his trauma. 'Not consciously. But I'd said I'd get him. He should have taken me seriously.' The schoolboy boast rang horridly genuine; his habitual benevolent smile was replaced by a vulpine sneer of triumph. 'It struck me on Monday night that this was the perfect time to do it, the one time when there were other people around with a wish to kill him. Tony's little tiff at dinner brought that out clearly enough.'

He did not even look at Harrington's former sales manager as he went on. 'I went back after we'd broken up for the night. Alison was having the devil of a row with Guy about him trying to put his hand up her skirt.' This time he did look at the person he mentioned. 'If my poor little Felicity had only been able to treat the bugger as you did . . .' The tears started anew. Alison Munro went and knelt beside him, taking a murderer's hand into hers as if it had been that of a harmless infant. Goodman stared down dully at his carefully manicured fingers, scarcely longer than Alison's own, as if he wondered that they could have wrought such things.

His voice as he went on came now in a low monotone, as if he were determined to complete this before exhaustion claimed him. 'He laughed at me when I mentioned Felicity. Said something about all being fair in love and war. Then he turned away and looked out over the valley: I remember thinking how brilliant the stars were behind his head. Perhaps he was a bit drunk. I waited until he was turning back to me and put both hands against his chest. He went over the edge without even a shout . . . I'm glad he's dead. I'd do it again, if I had the chance.' Even on this last assertion, he did not raise his voice above that awful uniformity.

There was nothing but sympathy for him in the room. Each of his four companions was glad that his victim was dead; not one of them would at that moment have raised a finger to bring him back.

It was Lambert who recalled him resolutely to different moral ground. 'Why Marie Harrington?' he said gruffly.

There were gasps around the room. All of them had heard of the second death; probably most of them had not until this moment connected it with Goodman. For a moment Goodman looked again as if he was not quite sure where the question had come from. Then he said, 'She knew. She would have given me away.'

No attempt this time to excuse the crime in moral terms, to offer any excuse for the darkest of all human crimes. Lambert was struck once again by the brutalizing effect of violence, so that a man who had wrestled for months with his personal agony before the first killing could offer no explanation of the second beyond the fact that the woman was a danger to his security.

As if to reinforce this view, Goodman said slowly, 'How did you know I'd killed her? Did she tell you about Felicity before I got to her?' There was still no hint of remorse: this time the whole room picked up that chill message.

Lambert said, 'No. Sergeant Hook saw her yesterday afternoon, but she tried to protect you. She pretended she didn't even know about your daughter. That was what pointed us towards you, in the end. When I talked to other people after her death, I found that Mrs Harrington not only knew Felicity but had been kind to her. That suggested that she had been covering up for you. We found out all about your daughter by contacting your wife and others in Surrey.'

Goodman looked bleakly round the faces of his friends, wondering which one had unwittingly given him away. For the first time she could remember, Meg Peters was grateful to the police for the anonymity Lambert had conferred upon her unconscious revelation.

At a nod from Lambert, Bert Hook stepped forward and formally arrested George Albert Goodman for the murder of Guy Harrington. The ritual of the words brought a kind of order to a room full of racing emotions. Goodman was taken away under guard. None of them said much, but none of them felt held any longer in that net of silence in which the revelation of Goodman's crimes had for a while enmeshed them. It was Sandy Munro who asked in his soft Fife tones, 'What will happen to him now?'

Lambert said, 'He will be charged and tried. What happens to him then is fortunately not my concern.' It was stiff and unsympathetic, but he was thinking of the unforgivable killing of Marie Harrington. Policemen were not automatons, even when the law demanded that they should be. He had liked the honest, spirited widow whose life had been so ruthlessly terminated. He would not readily forgive Goodman for that killing. No doubt the psychiatrists would get busy on a plea of diminished responsibility. At that moment, he was glad that his duties ended with the arrest.

Five minutes after Goodman had been driven away between two officers in the back of the white police Rover, his erstwhile

276

companions left the Wye Castle. The Munros and the couple shortly to become the Nashes were of very different temperaments and backgrounds, but they felt united by the touch of tragedy as never before. The Munros had already been cautioned: later they would be charged as accessories after the fact, though the charge might never come to court.

The two couples took their leave of each other in the car park, as if there was safety in numbers from the emotions which threatened to overwhelm them. Then they drove out behind each other to join the world they had left five days earlier.

Each of the four took a last look as they went at the rich English scene, with its majestic trees, rolling green slopes, and wide, unhurried bends of river. It was a scene which had changed little in centuries, and would scarcely do so during any of their lifetimes. It was undeniably beautiful.

But none of them would ever return.

We hope you have enjoyed this Large Print book. Other Chivers Press or G.K. Hall & Co. Large Print books are available at your library or directly from the publishers.

For more information about current and forthcoming titles, please call or write, without obligation, to:

Chivers Press Limited
Windsor Bridge Road
Bath BA2 3AX
England
Tel. (01225) 335336

OR

G.K. Hall & Co.
295 Kennedy Memorial Drive
Waterville
Maine 04901
USA

All our Large Print titles are designed for easy reading, and all our books are made to last.